W9-APS-101

DARKER WITH
THE LIGHTS ON

DARKER WITH
THE LIGHTS ON

STORIES

David Hayden

**TRANSIT
BOOKS**

Published by Transit Books
2301 Telegraph Avenue, Oakland, California 94612
www.transitbooks.org

Text Copyright © David Hayden, 2017
First published in 2017 by Little Island Press

The right of David Hayden to be identified as the author of this work has been
asserted by him in accordance with the Copyright, Designs and Patents Act 1988.

ISBN: 978-1-945492-11-2
LIBRARY OF CONGRESS CONTROL NUMBER: 2018934761

DESIGN & TYPESETTING
JUSTIN CARDER

DISTRIBUTED BY
CONSORTIUM BOOK SALES & DISTRIBUTION
(800) 283-3572 | CBSD.COM

PRINTED IN THE UNITED STATES OF AMERICA

9 8 7 6 5 4 3 2 1

All rights reserved. This book or any portion thereof may not be reproduced or
used in any manner whatsoever without the express written permission of the
publisher except for the use of brief quotations in a book review.

TABLE OF CONTENTS

DARKER WITH THE LIGHTS ON

Egress

MANY YEARS HAVE PASSED SINCE I STEPPED OFF THE LEDGE.
I cleared my desk, and all that I wanted to keep was
saved on a memory stick placed in my top pocket.
Everything else—I deleted. I found a window that I could
cut and cut again to make an opening through which I
could step out onto a narrow ledge, and as I moved from
there into the air I felt relief, a loss of weight. I began
to observe the office building as if for the first time: the
honey-coloured glittering skin of stone, the terracotta
panels, smooth and grooved; the sheets of clean glass. My
eye and mind moved with delight from the detail to the
great mass of the building and back again. I felt joy to be
outside forever.

I expected to be cold but the air was mild, the speed delicious, the freshness vast and edible. I remember looking
up briefly to see my fellow directors staring with alarm
through the boardroom window. All except Andrew who
pinched his tie, smiled and waved.

I stopped all of a sudden on the air, all my mass returned to me, seemingly in the pit of my stomach, my

arms and legs flopped forward, and I gazed down to see a woman with a chestnut bob staring up—I was definitely too far away to tell it was a chestnut bob. She looked away, down at her feet or towards the door of the yellow cab that had just pulled in to the kerb, and I began falling again as quickly as before; and the cab door opened and, as she stepped in, she glanced at me again, and again I paused, juddered in the sky, and I heard the door thump closed—I was probably too far away to hear the door thump closed—and I began falling all over again with fresh delight. I sang, and the stale, old words tore away from my mouth and up towards where my life had been.

Pages flew up towards me. I caught one and read:

Forehand cross-court, faster than the eye can see and he's on his knees crying, and the crowd are cheering, they are on their feet, and he's still on his knees grasping his head as if to hold in the burst, the spraying contents, and his opponent has jumped the net and is standing close to, watching the victor weep. The winner's mother and coach appear and stand around him and the weeping continues until the crowd falls silent. The defeated man steps forward and places his hand on the victor's curly head and he calms, stills; his tears cease.

The page left my hand.

I had the idea that I should be falling at a more or less constant rate, varying a little depending on how much wind resistance I presented by increasing or decreasing my surface area; but I found that I was accelerating. And yet, after a few minutes, I could see that the ground was farther away from me than I could have expected it to be and, what is more, seemed to be receding faster than the rate at which I was falling. I rolled over and the building was peeling away to the side and I strained, against the blur, to look in through the windows to the brightly lit, open-plan floors and I saw people held in tension, faces desperate, smiling, empty, fear-struck, fulfilled, turned away. Everything was as it should be.

Many gathered coats and bags and headed for the exits. A moment later they were pushing out of three great revolving doors that face the street on the ground floor. Going home.

Homes are places made familiar through returning. Time is inside the fragrance of return, and it is not freshly baked bread, not lemon zest, icy pine forest or mother's neck; it is not just stale coffee, stale smoke, stale sweat, the tang of detergents, or the rich, unnameable odours of the new, old, building reasserting themselves over, and through, the everyday fug; it is the substrate that we make, alone and together, out of the stew of chemicals that our skin encloses, out of the choices we make, or are made for us, about what we take inside, what appears outside, and everything that was there before us that still has a trace that can rise. The fragrance of return is all that we did, and was done, returning to us in a moment as the door opens.

Night happened without my consideration. The sodium orange street lights and palely fizzing moon appeared according to their different causes. On every floor were lone workers, spot-lit in their cubicles or at the desks of their private offices. My office, cool and comfortable, was up on high, towards the clouds. It was the perfect situation and moment and occasion for making money by making things happen. Each working hour like the beat of a heart, fast or slow, in sinus rhythm or bumpily asynchronous, entailed with all the others in apparent continuity, but each time gone and gone and gone and gone.

People like myself, whose long-settled routines determined their simplest choices, would be retiring to their beds and whilst I was tired it seemed risky or indecorous to fall asleep, to sleep while falling, and I resisted until the early hours when my eyes became the only part of my body to weigh, so far to say that I felt that they were pulling me to earth, orbs to orb. For a time, I was unconscious and dreaming—all useless things—and I woke in the dawn light reaching for a blanket that was not there, with a bladder big and tight inside my belly. I rolled over, unzipped and sprayed onto the street with relief, without regret. There was a larger movement inside and I pulled down my pants and strained it out of me and watched the brown stuff fly away and thump into the street where, I imagine, it broke into turdy pebbles. It was only when I pulled up that I chastised myself for an unclean act, and then I didn't think about it again.

The workers were returning, holding tall white tubes of coffee. They would join those who had stayed all night working on refractory problems, moving in minutely close or stepping back to a global distance to review risk or loss, to find resolutions that would cause money to leap free from wherever it was trapped: in bodies, components, minds or ore; in ideas, longings, irritations, bare possibilities. Everyone labouring to add more to the much.

The street was deep in snow: blank, then ridged and banked; grey and black and then clear. The bare boughs of the avenue trees sprouted curls of green that unfolded and spread wild, cloaking the wood, making buds and flowers and falling petals. The sun buried the city in heat; the star paled, lilac in dreams, scuffed yellow in the sky. The leaves turned sere, descended a scale of gold-orange-yellow-brown and flopped in fat, spicy drifts. Snow again and all was white, quiet, on the way back to green and gold and white. The smallest tremors of the sun on the air, the air pressing on the ground, the air pressing on itself—humidity from ash dry to falling ocean, heat searching and rising, swelling bodies and air. All days in one.

Cars appear bigger: shiny, brittle shells that move slowly, serried, similar amid their great variety; then smaller, faster, blips of light that never touch one another—fewer and fewer until the avenue lies empty of all moving things except the occasional ancient bicycle—rider bent over the frame, face covered in a surgical mask.

I roll and smile to the sky. Birds with mighty, cloudspanning wings gyre above, the sun flashes on their smooth bodies, and when I turn back I find I have dropped many floors and the ground is coming up fast. I close my eyes and count, running the numbers backwards. When I open them I find that I have dropped many floors and that the ground is coming up fast.

Many years have passed since I stepped off the ledge. All that I wanted to keep was saved.

The Auctioneer

THE CREATURES ARE ASLEEP AT LAST. One has been suffering from a colic and keeping the other awake with him. The auctioneer has brought blankets to ward against the night's slight inclemency and bedded down in the P quarters. The auctioneer has often said that he believes animals take comfort from a human presence in times of illness, as a child would. From my bungalow, in my armchair, in my sitting room, I can see the auctioneer's lamp blink and flicker.

When I first came to this country to join the company I was confused by the broken topography of the settlement. Even in the old quarter the streets are often unfinished; grand villas stand on their own in dusty paddocks, unconnected by path or lane to the main thoroughfares. Lanes end in boreens that slip into the compact, glossy jungle. There is one tall building in the town, the hotel, and from the roof one has the impression of an island that is sinking slowly, pleasantly into a great, green ocean.

When my wife departed I moved to this bungalow, which is very comfortable in a modest way. I prefer modesty now that humility has been forced upon me. The auctioneer arranged for a cash advance on the balance of those belongings that Ellen did not take with her and with which I no longer wanted to live. He believed that he would achieve a better price for the paintings and furniture at the twice-yearly metropolitan auction; and so it turned out.

I am grateful and I need for nothing. The auctioneer is a very kind man. Or perhaps he is not. I have no reason to think so either way. I should say, the auctioneer is a very thorough man.

I play my guitar at night and no one complains. The heat and the humidity make the guitar go out of tune but that is always temporary, one can always retune a guitar. I used to play a great variety of pieces but now I attempt just one: a Scarlatti transcription. Tonight I picked up the guitar and held it for a time, but did not play. Sometimes that can be as good.

My brother wrote me a letter. He wrote: "I don't understand how you can just not work. Do nothing. But then I've never done nothing. It would drive me mad. Perhaps you should . . ." Perhaps, I should not.

Often I sit rolling a piece of mental grit over and over in my mind, and sometimes it emerges as a perfectly rounded nacreous wonder; other times it merely grows into a larger piece of grit. Anything that shines I lock away.

This has nothing to do with my brother.

The light falls on the ground outside the P quarters and

into the bright stain staggers a raw strip of dog. I hear, or imagine I hear, first one and then the other creature breathe out heavily. The dog skitters away.

The auctioneer told me that he once wrote poetry under the name Bernini Folds. This was at university; where one might expect. I said, "Aren't you tormented with shame?" and he replied, "Of course, but not about the poetry." I said, "What were you in for?" and he said, "Archaeology," then he said, "You?" and I replied, "Geography," and he said, "A good subject for the lost." I thought, "I wish I'd stayed lost the first time."

Everything is still, or maybe vibrating only a little. The moment is better than bearable and the sour odour of the dusty night suggests the decay of the world has stopped at last. I cannot recall how or when Ellen left but I remember that towards the end her face had the look and smell of melting plastic.

I look down and my legs seem shorter, my hands larger, paler and fishlike. Life as it might have been. Whenever I imagine a knife, it is always a blunt knife. Whenever I imagine a drawer, it is a locked drawer. Whenever I imagine a meal, it is a cold meal. Whenever I imagine shoes, they are empty shoes. I like to imagine ordinary things; I find it calming. I don't like to imagine pink crosses in the desert.

I attended, not the auction for my goods, but the following one, out of curiosity for how they were disposed of. I travelled to the city by train, second class, which is as comfortable as one needs it to be. Hawkers appear at the appropriate times with delicious foods. In first class the time passes quietly; a sheltered journey to the hard end, and for them the food is no better. I had difficulty finding the auction rooms, which were much smaller than I expected and filled with an ebullient crowd of wealthy, shabbily dressed men, all of whom seemed to know one another. No one smoked.

When the auctioneer appeared everyone joined together in gentle applause as if for a chamber concert. He gave a slight, unironic bow, tapped his gavel on the lectern and introduced the opening lot.

"Lot one. Furniture from the office of the managing director of the Union Confectionery Company. A large studded leather sofa. A winged armchair, also leather, some ring stains on the left arm. A roll-top desk with stationery accessories: silver inkwell, black horn penholder, green leather blotter, et cetera. These items, attractive in themselves, present their new owner with the additional benefit of perfuming any living space, in which they are situated, with the comforting smell of caramel.

"Do I hear?"

One man nodded soundlessly, then another and yet another. The first nodded again and then the second and then the first again.

"Sold to the gentleman," said the auctioneer.

"Lot two. From the collection of the late chairman

of the Connolly Club. An exquisitely factored steel
kingfisher: requires repainting. A competent craftsman
will be able to determine the original colour scheme from
enamel flakes still perceptible on the surface of the bird
—or from life.

"Do I hear?"

He hesitated then raised his hand, palm out.

"No? Any private queries regarding this object can be
heard by me later in the usual place."

"Lot three. The final lot in today's programme—and
something both universal and unique. Lights please!"

Three assistants closed the curtains as a projector
beamed a hard square of light at the space over the auctioneer's head. He raised his arm, holding up a tiny silver
key tagged with a faded green ribbon. A slide appeared
of a man with a generous but well-shaped beard, frock
coat and top hat, smiling mildly.

"Sir Arthur Noone, known to us all, had a singular
collection."

Another slide appeared showing a tall, broad, terraced
cabinet with hundreds of small drawers.

"Collector's cabinet made from cherry wood with fine
tortoiseshell inlay, built by Brian Farnet to Sir Arthur's
exacting specifications for the purpose of housing his excrement collection. Sir Arthur throughout his life carefully
selected a representation of his most memorable movements which his valet carefully dried in the sun before

wrapping in Japanese tissue paper—Sekishu Torinoko Gampi, I believe—and laying in one of the drawers of this receptacle on a bed of green velvet."

A murmuring began amongst the gentlemen that could have been interest or disapproval.

"May I hear?"

The auctioneer scarcely had the words out of his mouth when the room rose in a great, shouting uproar. The assistants rushed through the room waving their white-gloved hands whispering "Gentlemen, gentlemen," and very soon the room was clear and we were alone.

"A successful event, don't you think?" said the auctioneer, although I did not know how he could be sure.

"Don't ask me about success," I said, and then at once regretted it. He looked at me, through me, for a moment. "Yes, a great success," I added to mollify him. We stepped outside into the high afternoon's furnace heat, the sky made violet-grey by billions of particulates cast upwards by feet and chimneys, cars and carts.

"Would you like to join me for supper? There's a quiet place I know near here." I assented and we walked past the plantation of stunted blocks that form the financial district. At its centre was our destination, a much older building, not much more than a large shack. The interior was harshly revealed by an excess of strip lighting, the moment we walked in the proprietor turned off a tinny radio that was seething with a horse race commentary. The auctioneer ordered for both of us and we ate in silence. I thought I would ask how he knew who was bidding what in the auction? How did they settle their accounts? How did he come to know this restaurant? What is the yellow dish with cashew nuts called? Who was Sir Arthur Noone? But his quiet absorption seemed to forbid it. Then I thought to ask him: Why did Ellen leave me? But only she could answer that. The silence was good, nourishing, or that might have been the food. In any case the quiet was not complete: every so often, the proprietor would pass through a curtain into a back room and as he returned to his place behind the counter his shoes would squeak on the linoleum.

We were waiting for more jasmine tea to arrive. I looked down to the plate, the cruets, the glistening table cover, the auctioneer's hands, nesting one into the other, tracked over and over in a fine tracery of red lines. He looked up at me.

"I have some expertise with flowers. A friend, a client really, asked me to untangle his rose bushes."

I had stopped thinking about his hands and was yet to start thinking about something else but must have looked puzzled because he added: "With the correct care roses grow well even in this climate. The stems were tough and the thorns as hard as horn, they bit me repeatedly until my hands shook but, in the end, I overmastered them."

"And the flowers?"

"Like blushing clouds of perfumed sugar . . . Although the blooms were a little large for my taste."

"And where is this garden?"

"I'm not at liberty to say."

The tea arrived and he relapsed into silence.

"I must go," I said at last.

"Yes, you must," said the auctioneer and he stood up abruptly and bundled us out of the restaurant, waving and smiling at the proprietor who mirrored his gestures, seemingly unconcerned that he had not been paid. Out in the street he took both my hands firmly in his and shook them whilst looking over the top of my head; then he threw my hands aside and marched off.

The journey back was the same as the passage out, except in reverse. I did not need to eat again.

• • •

I think about getting up, putting my music away, folding the stand, but I do not. Instead, I think at last of the afternoon I returned to the house after Ellen had left. I walked through the warped air of the hall and upstairs to her dressing room, not a place I had ever been.

Opening the double doors of her wardrobe, each giving a double crack, I peered in. Sandalwood, asafoetida, peppermint equivocated with one another in the air. Unsettled, I realised how tired my feet were. In the bottom of the wardrobe was a large, dead beetle on its back, a lovely shoe with a broken heel and a large bag, which crunched slightly as I lifted it onto the mattress that had been stripped of its bedding. On opening the bag, I saw thousands of bright pink, unspent, match heads, and thought about throwing the whole thing onto a fire, and imagined how it might fizz and roar, but I did not, then or later. I turned around and walked out of the house.

I slept in my office that night on the floor, and after dawn, long before my colleagues arrived, I cleared my desk, hand-shredded anything useful, and gathered a few belongings, which I placed in a box. That was my last day at work.

What was once fully there, absented itself over time in tiny increments, each one unnoticed by me. I recall now a fragment of something hard and white in the sink, something soft and torn and vinegary in the bedside waste-basket. A tooth, stockings, what I remember least.

The auctioneer is indifferent to objects, what he collects are the stories that inhabit things. He once said to me: "You know . . . I believe that we haunt our own possessions. They're dead, of course, but we are only slightly less so."

I muttered something about this being a very gloomy philosophy.

"Not at all," he replied, "being intimately involved with things that are more permanent than one's self is a lowering experience, in my opinion. The alternatives— flowers, food, wine, music—we have them, enjoy them and when they go we are still here, remembering. Few events give me greater pleasure than the demolition of a familiar building, fortunately a common event. Books might well be the worst of the household ephemera: dry husks that, slab by slab, rise in great, whispering walls, entombing their owners. The essence of the book is another thing entirely, not the words as such but what lies beneath the words, that is what can set you free. That is why libraries are so important, as long as one does not linger too long in them. If I have to buy a book I give it away immediately after I've finished reading. As it happens, I've just finished this. Would you like it?"

"What is it?"

He didn't look over to the book, which was sitting on the side table. "I can't quite remember but it's very good."

"What about people?" I asked.

"That's a very intimate question . . ." The auctioneer performed a very complicated gesture with his hands that I took to mean: Don't worry, I'm not offended. "People are, of course, a different category . . . aren't we? Famously both thing and 'not-thing' . . . I value both my mental confusion and the deep memories of the skin. What I most fear is being distracted by pain from what can be remembered."

I took the book home and it was very good.

I fall asleep in the chair and I find myself in possession of my power. I take what I need and the world loves me back; or it doesn't. I wake up to the sound of dry murmuring: my own. For a moment I am not sure whether it is day or night and then suddenly it is obvious. The night ages, its shapes changing, becoming heavier, more sudden, less and more reticent. After dark, what is known and separable in the daylight becomes parted from naming, becomes—even when illuminated—less securely knowable. The slope of the auctioneer's rarely driven car; the outhouse, abandoned since the arrival of indoor plumbing; the stack of paving stones intended for use in mending the broken walkway, but delivered damaged and never removed; the job, like so many, left incomplete. My eyes return to the outhouse, a happy sight, much homelier than the pretended sterility of the modern bathroom, whose only advantage is the absence of deadly insects. These days only neurotics are in touch with the passage of goodness through the body, its absorption and reduction into compact waste on its way to nothingness. We want to hasten, to sanitise the moment of expulsion, cast out our supposed corruption, deodorise our end times. I appreciate that most people prefer it this way.

The auctioneer told me that the ancients invented mechanical devices in imitation of the mind of the world. I said: "That's too vague for me. What ancients? What devices? What 'mind of the world'?"

"The mind that you sense when you become still . . . the mind beyond your own mind."

"That doesn't mean much to me," I said. "Most of the early devices that archaeologists have discovered don't seem to have a clear function."

"What about military engines?" he said.

"Naturally, war is a given. I mean the pure machine; it doesn't have to do anything . . . it just needs to turn over to tell us . . ."

"What?"

"That there are rules, dynamics, processes . . . operations . . . that they don't always work and that they don't mean anything in themselves."

"You've lost me . . ." he said.

"But I'm not sorry . . . given that you're still here."

"Thanks . . ." I said. "Thank you for that."

"Look, let's change the subject . . ." he said, "when did you stop running?"

"What?"

"I mean, you don't still run, do you?"

"No . . . No, I don't. I can remember running but I can't recall the last time I ran . . . as a boy, of course, down school corridors . . ."

"When you were expressly forbidden from doing so?"

"Naturally."

"But not recently . . . ?"

"No, but I think I still could if I had . . . if I wanted to."

"But you don't know for sure?"

"No . . . But knowing is not really important to me."

"Me neither."

Eventually I get tired of the mystery and suggest that if we are going to talk I prefer either silence or story, so the auctioneer tells me a story.

I was disappointed when he started by saying "Many years ago," but that was how the story began.

"Every day I used to visit a café in the outsiders' quarter run by a Roman called Dino—not his real name. Dino grew his own herbs, aubergines, zucchini, even mushrooms, although he would complain about mushrooms for hours given the opportunity. But this story isn't about Dino. This story is about a street performer called Paron. Every lunchtime Paron would run his act for customers at Dino's.

"Paron's act was as follows: He would stand statue-still until he had everyone's attention. Then he would start to talk very quietly, although with great animation; he gradually spoke louder and louder until you realised that he was telling a long and highly convoluted joke. He would end the joke and, without moving his feet, laugh with a kind of molecular-level vigour that I've never seen in any other person. Of course, even though no one had heard the start of the joke, and the punchline was never funny in itself, everyone laughed. It wasn't infectious as such, what Paron's laughter compelled was more a physical response, like crying when punched hard in the face. Then Paron's face would suddenly immobilise and he would cease all bodily movement before silently starting another joke, ending this time with an even more violent display of laughter before returning to his frozen state. Paron's third joke was all silence except for the volcanic eruption of laughter at the end. People would stand up, walk over to him and place small bills in his hand. Then he would go away."

"What happened then?" I asked.

"I stopped going to Dino's when I discovered how good the local food is."

"What happened to Paron?"

"Nothing . . . He died . . . He didn't die . . . I don't care. It's just a story."

I sit still and try to listen for the mind beyond my mind. I don't hear anything. I feel like a fool.

There's an unsyncopated rattling and stamping and a man comes into view on the street. He walks, white-robed, in front of a cart pulled by an ass that carries a large ironbanded barrel. In one hand is a bucket, in the other is a dipper, and in a rapid, regular movement he plunges this into the bucket and broadcasts a scatter of water over the dusty road. The water cart moves on and the smell of the night becomes danker, deeper.

Ellen's voice has gone. First, I lost what she had said, all those everyday weaves of words that make one belong or angry or lost. Then I forgot how she spoke: the pitch, the timbre, the rhythm. Maybe she was one of those people whose every statement rises querulously at the end, suggesting that everything is in question. I say something aloud; I think I might have forgotten what the human voice sounds like. I say: "Water doesn't run, it walks." Nonsense really, but it brings the idea of a voice back to me and I realise that there were moments when I grasped what she was trying to say, that it was important, that it would change everything, but none of this is available to me now. Of course, I can still hear her screaming, that's very clear in my thoughts, especially in a tranquil hour such as this.

The company, specifically my boss Simon Hollis, was not pleased with "my proposed departure" as he put it. "This is a role from which no one resigns. No one has ever left the company in this manner. I will, of course, prevent your departure from being generally harmful to the company, our clients or our shareholders, in an immediate sense, but I regret to say that I cannot protect your colleagues from the discomfiture of your selfishness." Simon had raised his voice; he ran his hand over his springy hair, head sloping to one side as he did so. "I understand that you've been . . . that . . . well . . ."

"Don't," I said. "You're not going to refer to Ellen. I won't have you . . . I won't tolerate it."

Simon sat back, he looked grateful for his desk. I thought he was going to cry or be sick.

"You've embarrassed me . . ." He swallowed thickly, I could tell he was going to ask me to get out, maybe even shout it.

"You're going to tell me to get out, aren't you?" Simon flinched like I'd made to hit him. "But there's no need, I'm leaving . . . that's the point."

Maybe I was smiling, I don't recall, Simon wouldn't look me in the face. I stood up and extended my hand to him over the desk.

I stood there for a long time but the next thing I remember I was standing outside.

• • •

The chair does not creak and, in any case, I have not moved for some considerable time. Against expectations the world around me has grown generally darker. The light must have failed again at the night market that is a short walk from here. For ten minutes, twenty minutes, my possessions lose a slight degree of perceptibility, then I realise that I can read the word "laughter" and a green number on a small, square paperback on the shelf across the room. The generators will have come on. The market never closes so I find there is no sense of urgency in shopping. I find that, apart from food, if I put off buying something for long enough, eventually the need passes. Some nights I wander the market as an entertainment.

Square aluminium poles framed together, thick plastic sheeting, chemical blue, cataract white, strings of bulbs and storm lamps—repeated hundreds of times. The rows, narrow, the stalls press into one another. The made, the remade, the broken, the faulty, the lost, the stolen, the adulterated; the priceless, the worthless, the bargain, the low deal. The searching, prodding eyes and fingers and minds, looking for purchase—looking to grasp what is needed, desired. Eager, desperate, indifferent, dutiful. Shopping. Do the stallholders make a living? A good living? Some carry their goods by hand or cart, rugs carried over warped shoulders, boxes of bright, poisonous toys; others drive imported cars with smoked windows, kidnap-proof locks and armed drivers. There are so many stalls that specialism proliferates. In a cluster dedicated to household goods there are a dozen knife stalls; one selling used medical equipment appears to do good business.

I look into the nothing that hovers in the middle distance between my chair and the walls, the window. I scrub at it insistently with something abrasive, submerged—not quite thought. A dozen kinds of nothing peel off one another before I am looking at Ellen again. The parts of her are centrifuging away from each other while holding somehow into one: still Ellen. My hands bunch up then release. I remember returning from a holiday at a friend's old mill house, carrying an already redundant typewriter—heavy it was too—and kilos of walnuts that we had gathered: a small surcharge for having stayed at a discount. Ellen was angry about this—the typewriter not the walnuts—and as the train pulled in we raced across the city to drop them off; I can't recall how it ended. Some people look more like themselves when they are angry. I can't say that Ellen did.

The picture of Ellen holds steady and I look into her

face, searching for meaning, but it doesn't happen. I wait for a smile to come up but it is still night. Night all the time.

One day last week I was walking in town and I saw a huge man swamped in an overcoat, its hem flapping up the dust, barrelling along, and holding—pinching—his elbow, was the auctioneer. He gave me a stabbing glance and steered the overcoat into, and across, the street. The next afternoon I saw the auctioneer on our road and he strolled up to me, and without any preamble he said, "You wouldn't have wanted to meet him. Believe me you wouldn't have wanted to meet him. I'm not apologising—just telling you what you need to know." He smiled and nodded, waiting. I couldn't think of anything to say, but didn't feel that I could leave. The auctioneer kept smiling and nodding, raising and releasing his eyebrows, until I felt that I was no longer there. I turned around and walked into my house.

What I see of my room and the world is changing as the darkness dilutes and the night starts its end. There is a dirty bathtub on the street that I did not notice before. Someone—some people—must have abandoned it while I was asleep. I can't help thinking that I would have cleaned the bath first. In an hour or so a man will come and quietly place a newspaper outside my house. I will turn my face away from the words as I screw up the yellow pages and put them in the range.

More of Ellen returns to me at this hour. Her form

remains static, poised. Her eyes come back stronger than the rest of her body: shining, searching, questioning. I can feel her hand in mine, cold and dry—perfect. We holidayed on the beach out of season. The northern ocean is all before us, roaring, calming. The wind's long, unimpeded journey ending on the shore with us. When I think about our conversations there all I can hear is the sound of my own voice circling around itself, elaborating tirelessly, marking you, blunting you.

The back of her head was inexpressibly precious to me then. I gazed at her, trying to apprehend her meaning to me and hold onto it forever.

At the time I thought I was losing—everything seemed so frangible and impermanent. I had no idea how fixed experience becomes when time has compressed its delicate grains into hard, buried blocks. I want the strata to be stripped back, the ocean winds to return and free my little substance, raise it back into the air and make everything possible again.

When the auctioneer valued our possessions he asked me if I was sure that I wanted to sell them all. "You will never see them again. Remember that. I am not one for holding onto things, especially when circumstances are trying to tear them away from one, but I do recommend that one keeps a small number of objects to help facilitate one's memory."

"What specifically are you referring to?"

"Well, her . . . Ellen's ball gowns. You could . . . keep

one." His voice had slowed to a stop. He looked at me nervously. The auctioneer started again, brittle, business-like, "The resale value is low—at least here—no one dances here . . . not in that way."

I told him I thought it was an awful idea, a catastrophic idea, and then I said: "The emerald gown . . . keep that one. If I need . . . that will be . . . that's the one."

He tried to shake my hand, put his hand on my shoulder. I pulled back sharply. I could see my own revulsion reflected in the dismay on his face.

This is the longest moment of the night, when the dawn seems to stall and the new day is at an agonising pitch of sharpness, undulled by repetition and the presence of people. I can read my room clearly now, and I feel the need to review my few remaining things and throw more of them away. The last rug, my dictionary, the corner table with its lamp; they have started to oppress me tonight and they must go. I do not want to go to auction. If I put them on the street this evening they will be gone by the next morning. Ellen is here, she is ready to talk but I will not let her. Time has run out and now it is drying up. Ellen looks directly into my face. I can't manage this so I look down at my hands; they are withered too. I am a coward. I need to stand up but I cannot, I look up instead and see her more clearly. She is my beauty. Everything comes together in her. Somewhere far away there is panic. Mine. This is the coolest part of the day. The dew has its moment before the light of the sun pollutes the sky.

Ellen is wearing an emerald taffeta ball gown; one of the heels on her lovely shoes is missing. I think to say, "I like your hair," but it comes out at a scarce whisper. Her eyes stay open; I'm not sure that she is blinking. There's a grinding, loud and close, shuddering my head; it's my teeth. It ceases and I can hear the creatures stirring. Soon the auctioneer will rise. Ellen stares at me patiently—no, tenderly—or vacantly. No, intently. She hasn't moved but she's closer to me, she's telling me. I am ready to hear everything but then I realise that all along Ellen has been screaming. One word. Screaming. Tearing out the word. One word.

Stop.

Hay

Andy straightens his hat and listens to the carriage song. Long metallic Es and F-sharps, grumble-rumbles and a *shack, shack, shack*. A pause and a *shack, shack, shack*.

Ochre light holds the interior still and suggests the great brown world outside. Andy shifts tackily on the beige seating. Everything exchanges the super-rich heat. Everyone is imperfectly at rest.

The train scutters over a long bridge that might have been an aqueduct in a country with water. Andy looks rightwards, out at the blue concrete towers that many people live in. The windows seem concrete too but they cannot be. The train rises to the height of the pyramid roofs, corrugated iron with verandas where people store boxes.

On one of the verandas Andy sees a man, a very young man with a beard. He is leaning backwards in a harness and the harness is roped upwards and as the man lifts his feet off the floor he starts to rise. Andy realises that the man is being lifted into the air by a bale of hay. An ordinary cuboid bale of hay. The man is rising slowly, looking down, keeping his rope clear and his harness steady. Always looking down but not noticing that the rope is stroking the rough edge of the iron eaves, and that he will surely collide with the roof if he does not kick against the wall or the post.

Andy looks away and leftwards to the packs of houses that lie under a different sky—dark blue, rippling. From the windows people watch the passing train, but they are small and Andy cannot see their faces. No one talks in the carriage. Andy looks at his own hands.

Looking rightwards again, the plain is clear except for a dotting of stunted farmhouses and the white sky-searching arms of the gum trees. Far ahead is an enormous tower block. No, it is a mountain-high stack of hay bales shifting from side to side slightly, slowly. The tower looms; it susurrates. Andy feels threatened. He goes to sleep.

Andy wakes up and the hay tower is exactly where it was, shouldering its mass in one place as if it has followed him. The train slows and slows and the song ends. Andy squeezes out of the narrow carriage door with his carpet bag and steps soundlessly onto the platform. The train is gone.

The sun is flat and white. The colour alone could make the world hot, even without its fire. Andy walks to the main street, walks past the tiled walls of the hotel and stops outside the café. A hand-painted sign outside reads: *Chew and Spew*. He steps inside. The café smells good.

"Long black, please."

"I'll bring her over."

Andy sits down on a detonated sofa in the shade. A blue apron shifts by. A man dips, shows his shiny head and wispy hair, and places the coffee on a low table.

"Food?"

"Maybe later."

The man nods, smiles to himself, and walks back behind the counter. He starts to polish a glass with his rubber.

"Aren't you hot in that suit?"

"I suppose I am."

"Did you need that waistcoat?"

"It goes with the suit."

"How's the coffee?"

"Fine."

"Do you mind the questions?"

"Yes."

"Why?"

"No reason."

"Food?"

"Maybe later."

Andy drinks two-thirds of the coffee hot, waits, and drinks the last third cold.

He crosses the street in the shadow of the hay tower. The office is opposite, behind a steel door. It is air-conditioned. Cool. Cold. The receptionist sits still behind her counter, not even pretending to type. She looks at Andy.

"Good afternoon," says Andy. "I'm here to see Krasczek."

"Krychek. He's expecting you. What's your name?"

"Andy."

"Andy, he's expecting you. Take the stairs."

"Why? Is the lift broken?"

Andy runs up the stairs and opens the door at the top. He looks out. There is a simple fall to the street. Andy runs down the steps, finds another door and opens it to find a mostly empty room with a man sitting on a large green leather chair with a stool at his feet. In the corner is a tough-looking yard brush.

"Mr . . . *Krasczek*?"

"Krasczek, yes. You must be Andy."

"Yes, I must be."

"Sit."

Andy steps forward and crouches on the stool. "The mine is flooded."

"*Flooded*?"

"Where did *that* come from?"

"The usual place."

"But it is so dry in these parts."

"Not in the mine it isn't. So the job is to make it dry again."

"Do you have any hydraulic equipment. Shinsky pumps? Outflow piping with secure attachments? Diggers for a run-off reservoir?"

"No, nothing like that, none of it is necessary. You just have to make them stop."

Andy looks at Krasczek silently, thinking: "Make who stop what?"

"Make the miners stop crying."

"But I'm an engineer. I don't . . ."

"How you stop them is not my concern. Stop the flooding is all."

Andy replies silently, inconclusively. "I'll pay you to try."

"I've never done this kind of work before."

"Try."

"Where's the mine?"

"I'll drive you. It's not far."

A snow-like rush of dust and dried grass sweeps around the bubble curves of the car. Scraps of hay and empty golden wrappers litter the floor. A sweet smell of coconut scents the air. Krasczek brakes suddenly and opens the door. Andy hears a faint tremor of moaning and steps out of the car. Krasczek is already most of the way to a large shack. Tiny pieces of hay shoot and swirl around, forcing Andy to shield his eyes, purse his lips and breathe through his nose. He begins to run, and reaches Krasczek as he passes through the shack's screen door. Krasczek shakes himself down and takes off a pair of protective glasses and a mouth mask that Andy had not noticed. Andy wipes his eyes and looks around.

The rise, rise and fall, fall of men sobbing finds a shape, each shudder mounting on the others.

One man stands in the middle of the room, water planing down his cheeks onto his twisting, outstretched hands. His fingers shine clean in the bare bulb-light of the shack. Another weeper stands in a corner leaning dutifully over a large tub that holds a flourishing bamboo plant. Dozens of men sit on benches at long tables eating identical meat pies with tomato sauce on top, buckets scattered at their feet. More sit at barstools gripping tubes of beer, the floor beneath them slippery with tears.

A solitary tearless woman moves up and down the room with a mop and bucket.

"It's bad."

"It gets worse."

"How did it start?"

"It just did."

"Have you called a doctor?"

"He just said it was idiopathic and started crying. Then he billed me for his laundry."

"Are all the women not crying?"

"Yes."

"Why don't you hire more women?"

"We don't do that."

"How come you're not crying?"

"I can't cry. I have to use tear drops."

Krasczek takes a golden envelope out of his pocket, slips out the rough, brown candy disc and pops it whole into his mouth. It looks uncomfortably large. Andy waits for him to swallow. Krasczek swallows.

"How long does it take for new miners to start crying?"

"Varies—usually about two weeks."

"How long does it take for them to stop when they're off the job?"

"Varies—usually about four weeks."

"Why don't you run a shift system? Two weeks on and four weeks off."

"That'd triple my wage bill."

"At least . . ."

Krasczek strokes the back of his head, grimaces and looks up.

"I can afford it. I'm already paying time-and-a-half tear money."

"Why don't you do it?"

"Because you've only just thought of it."

"What do you want me to do?"

"Well, I can handle the recruitment and the scheduling. I'd like you to survey the mine, see if there's any damage, and get it back to work."

"I'll do that."

Andy walks through the hay storm to the mine head, climbs into the cage, and descends. The hot soupy air shudders with sobs and low blubbing. The cage falls rapidly and rapidly slows before stopping. Andy rattles the gate open, presses the signal buzzer twice and steps out. A man with a long wet beard appears out of the gloom carrying a lamp and leads Andy down a narrow passage. The walls sparkle. The sound of men crying comes from every direction, growing louder as they half-run along with their necks craned to avoid scraping their heads on the roof.

Nearly an hour's walk later Andy sees an orange light up ahead. They are soon standing at the entrance of a great chamber. A thousand men are sitting or standing, alone or in groups, all weeping in their own ways, their silvery issue sluicing across the floor: a great self-syncopating orchestra of misery.

Andy quickly works out that standard pumping equipment will deal with the flooding.

"Is any work getting done?"

"Not much."

"Workings flooded?"

"Yeah."

"Why haven't you got pumping?"

The man wipes his beard and shrugs his shoulders. "How can you stand the noise?"

"After a while it's like it was always here."

"Why don't the men quit?"

"Pay's good."

Within two weeks Andy has a pumping rig fully operational. A month later the new shifts are working. There are so many men on the recovery shift that a large camp is built on the edge of town. At night the men go out into the desert to cry and drink beer. Dazzling flowers begin to rise up through the abandoned tinnies and soon the bloom is spreading outwards for miles around. Farmers move in and sow the desert with maize and wheat. Fields are planted with spinach, zucchini, pak choi and peppers. The growers reach an agreement with the mine to allow its workers to become shift weepers after spending periods of time underground. During the night they water the orchards of oranges, lemons, and mangoes with their tears.

Eventually the men desiccate and have to return to the city to rehydrate but there are always enough people to take their place.

Andy returns some years later and stays at the new resort hotel. He stands on the balcony and looks out at the gently shifting tower of hay. The sound of discreet crying arrives with the odour of ripening fruit, and silhouetted against the high, yellow moon is a solitary man held aloft by a bale of hay.

Memory House

THE MEMORY HOUSE IS IN MY MIND. Today and every day. Each thing is itself and is a way out to another object or to a time that happened or almost happened or didn't happen. I am the broken plate on the kitchen floor. Eight main pieces are grouped together on the yellowed linoleum that is cool beneath my bare feet. Scores of fragments are scattered in the greasy shadows, or wedged under the heels of the table. The warped, lemon-shaded light is my mother's eye. It gives off a gentle heat and sees nothing. Each chair is a misplaced friend. If I sit down I will remember who, and why they became lost and, perhaps, where they are today.

The table is a stony beach on a Cretan shore. Facing north, a salt-thickened breeze pushes back my hair. There are lights out to sea but none behind me. My baby boy rests warmly on my hip, his eyes narrow as he looks out into the future.

The mould-speckled draining board is just a draining board.

From upstairs I hear the blunt crack of steps on a

broken board. I should be alone here. I've always been alone here. But lately I've found evidence of a visitor. In the bathroom I found a damp, half-smoked cigarette in the sink. The sink is my broken tooth with taps for tears: hot and cold. I didn't see the assailant's face and I still wonder if he cut his hand.

The air smells of bay rum and sandalwood. I look into the empty bath. It is the smile of a girl I liked at school forty years ago. I open the window and the staleness is sucked out into the dark leaving the room cold and alert.

I'm on the stairs sounding like a horse, and then comes the kitchen.

From the shadowed pantry three white eyes stare out. They are flour, rice and sugar. Clouds of flour become thoughts cased in bone, grains of rice pulse out from my wooden heart through cracked ceramic veins, sugar crystals swell in my bladder.

I must go.

Down two steps, across the rushing carpet its pattern forming, distending and breaking. The floor beneath could be one great muscle. From the bottom of the stairs I am at the top with no motion in between. I follow the urinous smell to a battered door.

I pull the pure cord in the dark and something white and sticky pours from the ceiling; it is light. The cord is clean from the circular fitting at the top but halfway down turns brown, ending in a grey, plastic bell fragment.

I relax my muscles and micturate a stream of sugar into

the bowl, which piles up on the slope before slumping into the water. I shake and grains patter on the floor. The hair moves on the back of my neck, tall, dry grass, my head a rounded dune travelling slowly to the shore, a mud-choked littoral, the smell of ozone, sewage and tobacco smoke. I turn around to see a thin, white cigarette left on the top stair post, it is burning rapidly and by the time I am within reach it is all ash.

There is a clatter in the kitchen but from where I am I cannot move. Someone shouts and the sound billows out behind me then funnels away before sweeping back over my head and down the stairs. I follow, passing the mirror at the bend in the staircase. I look into the glass and a seagull gazes back: stone-blue pupils, yolk-yellow iris, beak wide open dripping black tar. I hiss back.

Downstairs the sea crashes against the windows, a pane shatters, the grey water plunges in then rescinds taking the glass with it.

All stills. In the kitchen a broken umbrella and belted raincoat lie on the table. I don't recognise them and return to the living room where I squat in front of the fireplace dropping coal in the grate a piece at a time from a galvanised bucket using a pair of brass tongs. The matches are damp but one flares and I start the kindling. Moonish smoke rises from the pyre and begins to fold on top of itself, layer after layer. I lie on the mossy sofa, a spring pressing into my back. The fire begins to roar orange and my fingers unclench in the easy warmth. Rolling forwards, one hand forks over my face and I sneeze, a green smile twitches on the floor like a tapeworm. The smile ripples towards, then over, the tiled surround, puckers slightly then kisses the hot coals. I hiss again, bitumen breath and a white gas cloud the size of a sugar cube puffs from my mouth. I put my hand behind my back, dig under a cushion, pull out a bag of broken biscuits and begin nipping off the hard pastel frosting. I throw the biscuit discs towards the fire but I miss each time.

The radio comes on loud in the yellow bedroom. I feel like my teeth are going to fall out. My teeth fall out and then fall back in again. I get up and the sofa's skin stretches and snaps back to itself. I stumble for the stairs. Light is washing and blinking around the trembling frame of the bedroom door. The handle rattles. I know I will be shocked if I touch it. There's a rushing sound behind me and I run into the bathroom waving steam away. The shower is on, yellow, green, red, silver sweet wrappers spray from the head into the tub and onto the floor. I close my eyes and grab the tap turning and turning, and when the flow stops I stand up and hear silence where the radio's clamour was. I undress and get into the bath, the heat and sweet perfume soothes me, frees me of the need to sleep that I have had for as long as I can remember. The dark, unfilled rags that are my empty clothes wrap around each other on the floor. I step back into them and walk into the yellow bedroom. A young, well-fleshed dog fox is sitting on a stool in front of the dressing table, its brush trailing on the floor. In the mirror I see the fox's jaw exposed, fizzing with yellow maggots, its eyes staring steadily, wisely into themselves. On the bedside table there is a glass full of water in which is a pair of dentures made with far more teeth than can be contained in a human mouth. A small metal box, a radio, shines next to the glass. I switch it on and there is a loud belch followed by a round of applause. I switch it off.

On the stool in front of the dressing table is a coat. From behind me there is a gagging then a throaty gurgle, a wet, chunky evacuation, perhaps through the nose as well as the mouth. On the bathroom floor in front of the toilet bowl lie strands of tomato and lumps of shrimp. I clean the floor and open the window, which slams shut immediately as if the outside air were resisting the gastric stench within. On the third attempt I manage to wedge the window open with a toothbrush.

I look up through the glass into the massing sky, bruised silver-grey and violet, and raise my arms, my hands, thinking through the sudden pain in my head, and see a frozen lark fall at great speed before exploding on the concrete path, scattering its music all around the garden in numberless, glittering fragments.

I open the back door and for the first time walk outside and when I look back I see nothing but trees. I sit on a rock and watch the nearest one to me. Silver bark crumbles from the trunk and snows onto the ground. The tree trembles.

I stand up in brilliant sunshine and turn to look over a rotten stile at a meadow that slopes away: long grass, scrubby, clumping weeds with tight pink buds, yellow butterflies twitch in the air, white mushrooms nose up through the damp soil, swallows dip and roll. In place of the sun a giant, golden, severed hand radiates in the sky. The hand closes into a fist making the world dark. Turning around, I run for the trees, eyes twitching up to the trunks and boughs that are scarred with hoops that glow orange ember. I trip over the step and fall into the kitchen smoke rising from my jacket.

The smell, like toasted marshmallows, makes me feel sick and hungry at once. I roll to my feet and approach the bread bin, carefully lifting the lid and, as I put my hand in, the loaf scuttles into the corner pressing up against the side, palpitating under the bag tie.

This is my hunger.

There are two foil trays on the counter with the remains of an Indian takeaway. The salad garnish has wilted but the food is otherwise good. I start to eat it with my fingers, the thick yellow sauce runs down my arm and I hold it at a distance for a while to admire the effect. I imagine that I have a fridge with a solitary cold beer on the top shelf. This is a good thought.

I put the hand under the tap and watch the skin turn

red. Walking quickly from the sink I step out of my shoes, they float away and I feel lighter and truer. There is a breakage far in the distance but still inside. The stranger is coughing and laughing in the parlour.

I reach the door, which gasps softly as I push against it and sighs as I pull it back. It may refuse to do this again.

I step onto an irregular orange rug, the burning sand cradles my feet, one move, two moves and I am struck by a jag of glass that pierces my foot to the pith and I stand bleeding freely. The desert turns red and I become blue while my foot pulses. I move off into a corner and reach for the floor, which spins around to meet me. Within reach there is a narrow bed and, propped next to it on its side, an empty television. I can't remember all the programmes I must have watched there when it had a screen but I know the time must have passed because here I am inside, looking at myself, watching nothing. I cough and, for a moment, I think I must be the stranger—I am a man after all—but I hear laughter outside the window, and then I think that he must be a piece of me that has broken off and is living a happier life than the one that I lead but, somehow, still cannot completely escape the original self who now lies maimed on the parlour floor.

But then I remember. I don't smoke.

I can't be the stranger.

The pillow ascends and approaches as if interested in my breath. It becomes as big as the moon; or maybe it is merely close and white and glowing cold like a pillow does before one falls into its plump, lightly wrinkled face with one's own red, heavily wrinkled, bewhiskered one. The moon or the pillow is behind me and my face is in front of me and the lack of a breath is not troubling me and I grow calmer and darker, waiting for the world to fall away not knowing whether it will fall up or down. I land heavily on my knees. (There will be a bruise.) The room shakes awake and I long for a blanket. I hear a long crisping sound, a suck and a pout, nearly silent, and a louder, but still quiet, exhalation, sour smoke drifts over my head and I struggle to stand, to turn, to see the secret smoker, to seize him—because it must be a him—to push him over, to crush his pack and kick away the yellow lighter, with its grinding wheel and shimmering liquid gas, into the shadows of the shadows under my bed where I will reach for it in the morning—should the morning come. I scramble sideways, pull myself up and balance on toetips, fingertips, before shuffling forward and rising in one long stretch. On the stairs I hear the rolling grind and solid *thump* and *thump* of a heavy ball descending.

I press my fingers into the palm of my left hand to dig out a chemical itch. I hold the sparkling hook in the air above my head before dropping it into my mouth and swallowing. There's a fishy wiggle and a tickle and then it's gone into the acid darkness.

There is a tapping under my feet, not on the plaster ceiling some distance below, but a hard, sore-knuckled rapping on the boards directly beneath the coarse leather of my shoes. There is a muffled shout from the same place; it must be hard to breathe there. I stamp my foot twice, three times and the sound stops. I fold over and put my ear to the warm wood.

The dark is hovering in the dark and behind these are the walls.

"Are you there?" I say but when I realise that I'm talking to myself I stand up.

Vines twist around the iron loops and knots of the bedhead. There is a force of sweetness passing through these living cables, swelling the grapes that group together and nod towards the pillow. Dragonflies rise and fall in the turbid air, rapid wings making a deep hum and I imagine that this is what makes my glasses tremble and slip down my nose. I go to lie down and I'm relieved to be that little distance further from the earth, pleased to be upheld, and I recognise the vastness of the effort required to keep flesh, bones, skin, frothing blood and the soft, thinking matter of the brain from parting, each from the other, and sliding into the soil.

I sense the possibility of no more happening. There is a sudden fall, a cough, of soot in the chimney and a small cloud passes over the tiles and settles on the carpet.

The stranger's sounds make sense for the first time. He is saying: "Get out of my house."

I turn around and a man is standing close to me swelling large on the in breath, shrinking and warping on the out breath. I talk and my words run backwards but I pull the sounds in and blow them out in the right direction.

"This is my home . . . my house. I have the deeds in my pocket. I always carry the deeds."

I hand them over for his inspection.

"You see," he says, waving the papers in the air. "I have the deeds. This is my house."

"But all of this is mine. It's what I've lived. Look—look . . . The rug there—it's the skin I tore from my back when I fell off my boy's scooter after steeping down a gravel path in the park."

"Everyone has skin."

"My books. All my books. I've read them."

"No one has the words. The mind is on a slope and the words run off like water and who knows where they go?"

"Not the words. The books. They're mine . . . Downstairs . . . in the drawer. The knives. They cut my food."

He has folded his arms and begun a slow, wet smile that I fear may never end.

"There's no food in this house."

I point upwards to the ceiling, his gaze follows and he cries out at the rough, fibrous shag of an over-roasted slice of beef; wet strings of fat hang down, bloody drops pendulate, hesitating to fall.

The stranger reaches over and returns the deeds. "It's your house. It is."

He stands wavering, thinning out.

"What am I doing here?"

"You've been scaring me."

"I was happy scaring you. I never thought that it was my house. I was lying."

"I know."

"I couldn't live in a house like this."

"Neither do I."

The stranger looks down at his shoes and so do I. They are just shoes.

"The truth is . . . I can't remember anything."

The Bread that was Broken

THE LEAVES OF THE TABLE had been folded out, grooves
and ridges covered with a bright spread of linen; fronds
of oak and acorn rising in a faint, silver cross-pattern.
Three displays of fleshy orchids—wet red, rubber orange
and albino white—were arranged in the centre, leaving
room for silver cruets and covered dishes that held a
variety of condiments: pickles, horseradish sauce, caper
sauce, piccalilli, salted lemons; with a space cleared for a
long, laminated cork mat. Each place was set with a half-
dozen knives and forks, lobster spikes, tongs and crackers,
spoons for soup and dessert, and a folded card on which
was written the name of each guest. New candles stood,
unlit, in their holders.

The guests arrived in pairs or singly, or coincidental
groups of three or five, the men in formal dinner attire,
their black ties neat or shapeless, the women all wearing
the same style of smooth and rippling, full-length gown
with a preponderance of scarlet, emerald, cream and
black. Mr and Mrs Hornsey, the hosts, smiled continuously and without effort. There was a degree of crowding

in the hall and the cloakroom as coats and scarves were removed and put away. "Does everyone belong here?" asked Mr Hornsey, and they all laughed.

White flames crowned the candle heads, a black and orange pyramid of coals cracked and shifted in the fireplace throwing out great quantities of heat. Fourteen bottles of red wine stood in a large bucket of cool water that rested on a white towel on the sideboard. There was a short, dry knock and Mr Hornsey stood up to hold open the door. Four men, white shirts glowing against black aprons, carried a long steel tray shoulder high towards the company. The guests parted to let the men place the tray on the central mat. A fierce, continuous hissing came from the great platter and a dense weave of odours: scorched wool, bad fat, warm urine and excrement, and the bitter, chemical stink of blood. The bearers stepped away from the table. There on the platter was the blackened, smoking corpse of a man. A green felt hat was beside his neatly oiled and parted hair, the face sunken from the brow to the chin down two-thirds of the left-hand side; a white gash of jaw and blackened teeth showed like the fragment of an unending grin. The remains of a heavy tweed jacket clothed his upper half, a copper counter-thread visible in the mossy patches of cloth that cleaved to his shoulders and elbows. Brown and bloodied bows of ribs showed through with most of the viscera missing. His arms and hands were raised and rigid like a pugilist hare's, the skin and bent fingers a glossy charcoal. A big-buckled leather belt was there unharmed but the trousers were tattered. The place for his sex was exposed but dark—the organs gone. The knees ridden up and slumped to the side, the right cap smashed and the shin beneath exposed: clean, white and hairy. Tan-coloured, mud-covered brogues were on his feet. Delicate alpine flowers were strewn all about the corpse, pale yellows, mauves and pinks, tiny tongue-leaves of green and threading stalks making a gay circle.

A place card rested on a white china saucer near the body's feet, on which was written: Thomas.

A sound began, a windfall pattering onto damp ground, the guests rapping spoons on the table, tamping heels on the carpet, tapping toes on the footrest, all of which gradually passed, merging into the murmur of revived conversations, bright, new chatter, chortles, giggles, bronchial coughing and, concealed in the admixture, several portions of sociable silence. "I learned nothing there and I fully expect my youngest boys to do the same. There is plenty of time for knowing later," said Mr Hornsey, his hands red and empty on the table in front of him.

Mr Decaux replied in a low buzz and Mr Hornsey's great voice rose again over the table.

"Rex and Donald will not have any problem with competition, Peter, if their feral natures are not too constrained with petty objectives—sticking coloured pieces of paper onto other coloured pieces of paper and the like. I am content for them to play sport through which they can distinguish themselves, or not, in ways that do not stand out from what can be expected."

His voice lifted a semitone.

"The claims made for sport regarding character are generally excessive and can be easily disproved by reference to the disordered and shabby lives of our professional sportsmen."

Mr Hornsey breathed in loudly and made a noise, part sigh, part moan.

"Moderation in everything . . . excluding moderation," said Mrs Hornsey, provoking most of the guests to laughter. She turned to talk to Miss Weston, who was seated on her left, gathering the great force of her beauty before she spoke. "I rarely stop. Stop fully and completely. And I find that when I do it tends to make me feel sentimental, as if all the excess emotion of life had caught up with me in one sudden, tidal moment."

"Oh," said Miss Weston, looking around at the door, the fruit bowl on the sideboard, the glass case empty of its dinner service.

"It's not unpleasant," said Mrs Hornsey.

Miss Weston's mouth shrank and puckered before she spoke.

"I prefer to use up all my feelings as they arise. I can't bear to feel bloated in that way. I mean . . . I just want to pass on to the next good thing."

Mrs Hornsey smiled, her round pink face lit up with doubt. Miss Weston began again.

"I don't see why that's so strange. Most people want to stay where they are. On the surface. Happiness is not possible in the depths."

"That's quite true," said Mrs Hornsey, "but it's impossible to sound sincere saying so. But you mustn't take that the wrong way."

She touched Miss Weston's hand and smiled. "You are quite charming, Mrs Hornsey."

"That's a dangerous remark."

"I didn't mean to be dangerous."

Miss Weston pulled her napkin further up her lap as if it were a blanket.

"You were not," said Mrs Hornsey.

Mrs Hornsey looked directly at Miss Weston, opened her mouth and placed a forkful of food inside. She slid the fork out, chewed, swallowed and smiled again.

"Can we stop talking now?" said Miss Weston.

Mrs Hornsey turned her back on Miss Weston and stared at the guest on her right.

The dark was outside, thick and blue, while in the dining room light glinted off silk and silver becoming a general glitter that, if seen from the night, would have signified a happy party.

Thomas's remains cooled and cracked, drew together, his legs turning further into the tray. A pale blue smoke hung in the air, which to some may have smelled of pork and, to others, could have been the unnameable odour of any unfamiliar home. "I feel like dancing," said Mr Decaux.

"You bloody fool," said Mr Hornsey, his face roaring with good humour for a moment before falling still.

The talk sped up, the meanings mostly indistinct, the sounds churning and looping, jolly and metallic. The ruins of old courses were removed and plump, glossy new courses took their place.

"That's a good feed," said Mr Clarke.

"I like an appreciative animal," said Mrs Hornsey.

Mr Clarke stopped and beaded his eyes at the hostess. "And what do you mean by that remark?"

"There is too much elaboration in our appreciation of food. We, who merely eat and drink, should leave that to the makers—to whom our thanks and blessings."

She raised her glass and the company raised theirs murmuring, "Blessings! Thanks and blessings!"

Mr Hornsey closed his eyes tightly for a moment, blinked at the room as if surprised and began eating again.

"The simple terms are best because sincere and most readily understood."

"That's me told, I suppose," said Mr Clarke, who returned to his plate.

"My husband whenever he opens his mouth finds a small, stale place there which he needs to fill with something: food or drink or, once upon a time, a cigarette. Or, at times and places that I can't often predict, he wants to stuff the hole in his face with one of my breasts."

Mrs Hornsey placed her hand under her left breast and raised it slightly.

Mr Clarke put his knife and fork down, turned

himself in his chair with some difficulty and stared at Mrs Hornsey's breasts with an intense and melancholy avidity. He bit his upper lip briefly and made himself look, not knowing what was there before him or in his mind. He looked until his face discomposed completely and he had to turn away.

"But most of the time he merely pushes the air out with whatever words he has available and one construction leads to another and, before he knows it, he's talking on and on, not caring whether anyone is listening or not. He's not above contradicting himself which he does with especial vehemence."

Mr Clarke looked at the space he had cleared on his plate.

A blue owl stared back at him.

"You don't think that you're being disloyal to your husband by speaking in such a manner. Do you?"

"Not at all. All men are like this. And I wouldn't have you questioning my loyalty to all men, Mr Clarke."

Mr Clarke raised his head a little giving her face a half-glance through his eyebrows to determine whether or not Mrs Hornsey was smiling. She was not.

In the dining room, the heads faced out to the flaming candles, knives cut, forks pressed, mouths opened, bodies filled with food from the gut to the craw, drink was tipped and fell in. The guests were calmed and charged, they luxuriated; the dinner enlarged what was already there.

Thomas had nearly cooled and a pool of his fat was growing visible by becoming white as it set. His wrecked eye and his good eye both blind, his brain complete and darkened, all electricity gone and with it the mind. The mind that knew, or thought it knew, the purpose of taking a daily walk, of a regular haircut, of holding open a door to a woman and nodding slightly as she passed to own, momentarily, whatever faint perfume might be on the warm air closest to her hair or neck. The purpose of being Thomas. Miss Weston shuffled back her chair, bunched her white dress between her legs then reached forward pinching the steak between her thumb and forefinger, raised it from her plate, grabbed a knife and scraped the Diane sauce onto the floor splashing her silver pumps. She rattled forward the dirty plate, placed the steak on the clean platter underneath and lifted the lids of a number of dishes around her until she found the garlic butter, which she spread in a thick layer on the meat. Miss Weston looked around and Mrs Hornsey was approaching with a steak knife and an open bottle of red wine.

"This is what you were wanting?"

Miss Weston tilted her head back and gazed at the plaster ceiling rose with its pure white grapes; the flowers and foliage that seemed to wave and dip in the trembling candlelight. She rocked forward, began to cut and stopped.

"I meant to say 'thank you.' I mean . . . thank you."

"That's quite all right. I mean to see you eat well."

Mr Decaux had become recessive, and with the force drained from his form the ghost of a slump could be seen on the left side of his body—a slight hooding of his eyelid and a descended cheek.

"This is who I really am. I'm better off like this, waned honestly with no prospect of a big show or a full face or a fine young tongue; clean and unbuckled."

"We're all consequences at this stage Peter."

"True but not well. Not well at all. I don't want to be part of the near-dead. I love the small flame of life I have left in me and I fold myself around it when I'm alone, especially since Yvie left me."

"Yvie was . . ."

"You tell me? What? To see me angry? That's long gone. I know what I lost. I know what I did."

Mr Hornsey's mouth opened and closed without words. "I had no notion that tedium would grow inside me, a slow contagion claiming every cell until it reeked from my pores, poured from my mouth, squeaked out of my sagging arse. Mockery was such a joy when we were young. You . . . you're still young."

"My wife, you know."

"I know."

Mr Decaux sat up straight and rubbed the side of his head with the heel of his hand.

"Soon there'll be cake."

"That's good," said Mr Decaux.

One of the black-aproned men returned bringing six green bottles. He cut the foil, removed the corks and placed the wine on a small trolley which he wheeled to the far end of the dinner table where a group of men sat, faces white and sweaty, ties askew, the top buttons of their trousers undone. The men cheered and each had a new glass filled, frothing red, to the rim.

The man waited behind them and replenished each glass as it emptied and soon the bottles were drained. He returned the bottles to the trolley and left the dining room.

The cheer fell from their faces and the men began to sing all at once. Although everyone knew the words, none of the other guests joined in. The tune flattened until it stretched out into one long note, passed from one man to the next, through which the words were declaimed.

The serving men piled into the room laughing and talking loudly and took the plates and platters, the glasses and bottles, the dishes and the cutlery, grabbing still-laden forks from the hands of the guests who were busy eating, until all that was left on the table was the flowers, the candles and Thomas. The singing rose over the clatter and, shortly after the men left, stopped.

Mr Hornsey spoke.

"I received a letter this morning," he said, "and it was full of . . . sounds, words. Words that, if one was to hear them aloud, would break one's ears. And everything . . . everything in between. Even on the page they were loud beyond comprehension the first time I read. And I read with my hands over my ears singing out as I used to sing him nursery rhymes":

In the dark above my bed
The golden light of day is set
To fall upon my baby's head

Mr Hornsey swept his hair back with a hand that trembled slightly.

"He wrote about being burned alive, which is impossible because one can't write and burn at the same time and then how does one post the letter?"

"That's a relief," said Mr Decaux.

"But it was true and he said that it was I who kindled him, that others had broken his body, but that I'd set the flame. We've all forgotten about him and he is here and we've all forgotten and we cannot see anything. Can't you see?"

Mr Hornsey's face had broken into unrelated pieces in the midst of which his eyes could see more than they could bear.

Everyone had fallen silent.

There was a knock on the door and a servant entered carrying a wooden platter that held a long, soft loaf of bread. The man set it down on the floor, kneeled and began to tear the loaf. He stood and walked around the table and each person took a piece. He placed the platter on the sideboard, picked up a candle hood, extinguished each of the flames until the room was as dark as the blue-grey night outside, and left.

"Is anyone still hungry?" said Mrs Hornsey.

"Yes! Yes!" the guests cried and began to bite and chew at the bread.

Mr Hornsey stood up shaking, threw his bread on the table and walked around to the tray where Thomas lay. He leaned over and stroked his cold head.

"My son."

Mrs Hornsey stood and placed her arms around Mr Hornsey's shoulders and the guests stopped eating and bowed their heads.

Leckerdam of the
Golden Hand

MY NAME IS LECKERDAM and this is how my children
killed me.

I was lying on the floor in my overcoat, drunk and rag-
ing, when my daughter Liotta appeared from the shadows
beside the fireplace and tossed a bucket of white ashes
into my face. I was blinded. She shouted "Anderdam!
Anderdam!" I scooped the muck from my eyes, regaining
my sight in time to see my son lift a coal hammer as high
as he could; its broad, steel head swept down. I turned
away and it struck me on the nose which tore off and flew
into the fire where it settled, sizzling. Liotta hit me on the
head with the bucket so hard that I span and slapped onto
my back. Anderdam stepped forward and began striking
again and again at my shins, my knees, my thighs. He
worked up my body, breaking, shattering. He broke my
ribs as if they were kindling. Blood sprayed hot and sour
into my mouth. I felt pity for myself. I was not ready to
die.

I stripped the glove from my left hand with my right
and raised it with the last of my strength so that its

flawless mass could shine in the orange firelight, could draw all eyes, all minds to itself—my golden hand—from wherever they were in the room. But my son merely lifted his hammer once more and struck me a final blow—a powerful one for a boy his age—my skull cracked like a crab shell and my brain was destroyed.

Liotta lay a blanket next to me, Anderdam rolled my body on top and they wrapped me up, tucking me in neatly. The children each took a lever, jammed them in the groove that runs between the floor and the hearthstone, and with great difficulty raised and slid the slab to reveal the mouth of the pit underneath. They each took a foot and dragged, then pushed me over the edge. I fell heavily into the ash and dust and lay there twitching and leaking.

The hearthstone was shoved, grinding over the floor before thumping back into place, leaving me alone and dead in the warm dark.

• • •

My children are mine.

On Liotta's sixth birthday I tired of her as she was— happy, celebrating, being celebrated—and with my golden hand I took a hot coal from the fire and pressed it to her forehead. She screamed, of course; she has always had a beautiful voice. The scorch was deep and left a wound that never quite healed, that wept continuously—unlike her eyes, which never shed another tear.

She asked me, "Daddy. Why why why why why why?" But that was just her age. I raised my hand and she stopped. Anderdam is a great boy—a grand, strong, rousing, sporting, cheering, contending, unthinking chunk of boy. He outran the hounds when he was seven, and when he was ten he hurled a stone over the wide lake and the dark woods, over the fields and the weed-strewn strand, across the seething sea to the island where it struck sparks on the roof of the old tower which, catching fire, burned all away. First I bent his throwing arm and then his left leg, and then I twisted his head so that it would not sit right. Anderdam opened his mouth to make what he could of his new deformity but nothing sounded. He has been wordless ever since.

From the dark and the warmth under the stone I can hear the rumble and crack of the fire. Anderdam and Liotta will be seated close by, she will be leaning forward from time to time stirring the supper pot; it bubbles and farts, loaded with carrots, potatoes and thumb-sized pieces of fatty pork. Soon they will eat the stew from two big, brown bowls, dipping their faces into the savoury steam, sucking up the stock from their spoons, chewing the good meat.

There are small creatures down here that scuttle over what is left of me. Great crowds of bacteria had bloomed in my corpse, feeding on me, wasting my substance, raising a stink for a while before dying away. I still have the desire to gather up my bones, to dispose of them in various poses; to dance, to fight, to feed, to fuck, to punish.

Although I no longer have the flesh to pull my sticks around, I have this voice and whatever it is that digs down into this pit of words and the pit itself, which is almost a body. The golden hand lies with me in the dark, the fingers twitch but that has nothing to do with me.

When I was a young man I left home, with its filthy corners and broken furniture, its inward-turning eyes and low sobbing, and I went out in search of a purpose. I turned my back on the woods, where foxes wept and owls barked and the charcoal men wandered in the shade like dark, friable ghosts. And I walked into the city, where the lights deafened me by pushing their small points into my eyes, large blocks of colour, and no-colour, made the blood in my eardrums quicken, thicken. The sounds blinded, my eyes shuttered at the shouting, grating, breaking noise of the streets, the shrieking steel of the elevated railway, the scattered horns of the massing, surging traffic.

The mud and the brown and the green of the country made me sink into the shit of myself but the heavy city, with its hard, clear edges, let me float and separate, disarticulate. Flopping down into a heap of thoughts and signs and desires that was matter that didn't matter, a giddy, accelerating swirl that felt joyful and pointless. I followed a man down the street. Other men followed me. We all walked up the crumbling steps of a liver-brown house, the door blackened steel, the windows black and blinded. The men, and I a man too, gathered in a large basement room with drinks, with music, with sparkling coloured lights, with comfortable chairs, with a giant pair of legs sticking out of a plain grey wall, with everything that you can find between a woman's legs. The feet kicked and scuffled on the tiled floor as the men, one at a time, dropped their pants and did their business.

I waited and watched. A janitor appeared, mopped the floor and left.

Everyone stood around laughing and joking about the legs, mocking the feet, the toes, the candy-pink paint on the toenails, the hairy sex. I thought that they might start dancing but that would have been wrong. I stood up, noticing my clothes for the first time, and I walked across to the wall. I checked the legs to make sure that they were not my mother's and I pushed my hand into her and kept on pressing until I was in up to my elbow. My arm warmed, became hot and then hard but still mobile; I could ripple my fingers. I pulled out and every man could see that I had a golden hand.

A blank, white light now governed my mind, agitation my heart, bitterness my tongue, folly my judgement, pride my shame and rage my overpowering hand. I had perfected myself.

At once, in the street people recognised my distinction and wanted to name and approach me and my various powers of inversion, diminution, unlearning, distraction; their jaws swung loose as if broken, jabbering to me as I passed: "Reach me! Reach me!"

These were the unpained. Those who already lived with pain—the burned, the shattered, the eaten-alive—sensed the possibility of notpain without knowing the terrible, unbalmable itching that would take its place.

I found a great square with a park where some people played chess, some roller-skated and others sold or bought puny drugs.

A crowd gathered around me muttering. I breathed in the air. A good, full smell like a clean butcher's shop. A policeman approached, his gross body swaddled in a too large black uniform, his gun a piece of sweating licorice. A lean man in a silver-grey suit with the face of a flayed dog pushed him out of the way.

"I am the mayor." He made a smile that didn't cover his whole face. "You may kill whoever you wish except . . ."

I caught him by the throat and squeezed once. The mayor burst and slopped to the ground. The police officer kneeled and kissed my bloody hand. I looked up through the waving branches of the plane trees at the sun and closed my eyes. I was expecting silence but pushing through the small circle of quiet that surrounded me was the boring, irregular clamour of the city.

When I opened my eyes the crowd was still there, looking at me, expecting more. I thought for a while of killing again—how that would feel, what it was for, what it would mean—everyone began to look like corpses waiting to fall.

I realised that one body was enough.

I took a newspaper from a bench and wrapped it around my arm and the crowd soon went away. I was free to walk the streets, to enter and leave my apartment, to steal from the stores, the galleries, the museums; to eat uncharged in the cafés and restaurants, to drink in the bars. I rode the subway, the cabs even, and on one occasion, a passing limousine that carried a couple in tuxedo and ball gown. I took their diamonds and dress watches and threw the partygoers out into the ochre snow, sitting with the door open for a moment while I laughed. I asked the driver to go round the block. I gave him the glittering junk and went down the steps of another bar.

Everyone except the bartender turned to look at me as I walked in. Everyone looked away again except for a woman in a blue, plastic dress sitting on a stool in front of a zinc counter with a full shot glass and a pack of cigarettes. As she gazed she grew larger and began to shine with a harsh, white light that illuminated itself and nothing else.

"I have almost everything I need," she said. "What are you for?"

I showed her my hand. "That's new."

"I'm leaving the city."

"You're not in the city."

"Are you coming with me?"

"Are you?"

Her name was Hannah and I became her husband.

We boarded a train for the end of the line and many hours later stepped out with the other passengers and their trunks and goats and chickens. They quickly disappeared.

The land was mud. Cold and green, it stank of slurry. Hannah and I had nowhere to live so we looked to the horizon and found the darkest point and walked towards that. Our bags became burdensome and we dropped them on the dirt. The sky lowered and spat ice at us. Hannah spat back, the sun came out and we were home. A cabin, that we took as our own, at the edge of a wood as wide and dark and full of death as the sea. The bed was narrow so we made our children on the floor. The years of infancy were sleepless and shit. Hannah ground out her teeth as the children nursed, spitting the fragments into the fire, and when the enamel was gone and her beautiful mouth was all stumps she got to her feet and spoke.

"I give in. What's mine?"

"Nothing."

"I'll take that."

And she walked out.

• • •

My children are mine.

I can hear them above. Liotta crying because she can. Anderdam talking, his tongue unknotted but thickened and halting, becoming reacquainted with the peristaltic push of words from throat to mouth to air.

Now that my children can live outside my hate I know that I am dead.

Limbed

CORNFLOWERS, eye-blue, heartsease, winking violet, delphiniums, risen purple, primroses, tooth-yellow, upgazing, sightless, calendula stars, thyme, tight green spicing curls, daisies, scattered wings, open palms; over all, fattening bees swing boozily in the warm air.

A journey of light ending and ending and everything feeding off this, in one way or another, with light arriving, warm and buttery, letting us see: shapes, shadows, colours and a cottage and a field and a cottage garden.

A man or a woman stands smiling once upon the day. All the motion of the living world above and the worm-turned earth below and the breath of life rushing from warm to cool, from damp to dry, adds up to a seeming stillness, a closeness to silence in which one may be wise, be idiot, be almost nothing. If not for the faint tapping heard and then not heard and then the man—it is a man—turns to the sound, which is where it is not, and turns again, to where it is not, and turns again; but the knocks have stopped.

He sits on a cool, slate bench and pulls on his socks and boots, then, standing, raises a left-hand L of thumb and forefinger to the white O of the sun, and reaches around the sky with the memory of the sound and, again, it comes as a *tap, tap, tap.* Across the field Lo walks, crossing ridges of newly turned soil, birds dip their olive beaks and lift their pied tails—hopping, swinging, flighting ceaselessly, feasting on tiny seeds and beetles.

Heat rises from the dirt in broad waves that are visible, not in themselves, but because Lo's sight through them is warped and rippled; nothing solid moves, nothing at all. Noticing this Lo stops and considers his clothes: green, heavy, folding over his mass, touching him in a way that could be disallowed as excessively intimate, as meaning that things have claims over selves that they should not have; but they do. And a *dat, dat, dat* sound; only a little louder given the distance he has travelled. The sun is in itself, pressing hard against the sky, being orange, and beneath, at the field's end, a copper river runs—loud at once, thick and reaching up its banks—there are ranks of sharp, black trees beyond this and beyond and beyond a blue mountain dabbed on the horizon.

Lo walks on and sings and the words run backwards out from his mouth in coloured ribbons and back into his mouth; or so he sings, the song being a song of a voice both pressing outwards and being drawn from the air, taking its many textures and scents and shaping words from there that fly out in coloured ribbons. The words are: "One day I will be." There is no melody as the words are both words and music.

He raises his hands, palms out, and falls flat onto the river still singing and is carried across on the fast flow of thin mud, sticks, window frames, fenders, boots, dresses, disposable razors and long-playing records. He rolls his body and stands, dry, on the other side where the earth is blue.

The black woods shoulder together, swaying and cracking; from time to time they flash white with lightning. Lo skirts the trees, averting his eyes but seeing the blanking seizures reflected in his polished boot caps.

There are no roads and Lo has gone past his furthest boundary. The land out here is untilled. On the surface fragments of porcelain, shards of twisted metal, chunks of masonry in blocks and cones are risen in the dry ground; where the land falls away irregularly are great circular hollows filled with putrid green water, floating over which are violet clouds of midges that gather round his ears and neck, dancing on their tiny feet. They do not bite. Lo stays his hand, deciding neither to kill nor provoke them, and as he passes by the sound returns. This time wetter, as a *thap, thap, thap*.

Lo hears the gasping and slurping of feet or mouths— many of each—two to one—but he sees no one except what he imagines of the many, many people striding sexless towards the mountain and Lo wonders if he might be one of these phantoms. He senses his head thinking, his trunk big and loose, his delicate fingers flickering at the ends of his arms and decides that he is curious: real.

The wind works percussively through the grasses, short and tall—a music complicated enough to seem random, progressionless, alive, machinic, marine, unintended: restful. The air changes direction and there's a sudden stink of estuarial mud. Lo looks around even though he knows the river is behind him. Gulls are nowhere in sight but he imagines their white evacuations falling from the sky, their cries, cracked, trapped in a bottle, the tips of their hooked, yellow beaks stained scarlet-orange. Lo turns the sky over by lying down and the grass sizzles and the not-there gulls grow frantic and silent; as the birds wheel above, their stone eyes shrink and tumble from their sockets, scattering down into his hair, eyes and mouth. Lo rises spitting out the eyes, and at the end of the sky sees three mountains, not one, that might be purple or red or brown.

Lo's first new steps are loud and beyond them is the skitter and pound of other feet and a long, wavering roar. On a large green, boundaried with long, proper lines of white paint, people become more and less themselves by gathering as a crowd, shouting, and on a small platform, like a table, draped with a pale canvas, like a tablecloth, two women, naked but for black aprons tied in front with red bows, face each other stamping their feet and grunting. One slaps gently, more a stroke; the other floats a measuring punch towards the chin and withdraws her arm. The women each make a solid, low, broad-legged stance a few inches apart from the other and begin to rock from foot to foot in a counter-motion, shoulders rising and falling, breathing irregularly through the nose and out of the mouth until they find each other's rhythm. The crowd silence themselves.

The women belt each other with well-moulded fists, left then right; skin bursts around the eyes and cheeks, lips split, noses crack, creamy blue-white milk pours down their heads and arms staining their aprons. The crowd are screeching and crying like colicky babies. They fail to make words.

The punching is heavy and continuous and the canvas becomes soaked, the milk washes to the edges and the spectators get on their hands and knees and crawl forwards, pushing their heads to the platform and, with teeth and gums, clamp to suck. They settle and quieten.

There is room for everyone.

Lo gazes up and sees a woman taking off a black apron. She looks tired.

The canvas is dry. The crowd stop sucking and stand up one by one and turn towards the mountains and the *chab, chab, chab*.

"I worried that I'd be overdressed," says Lo. The woman looks down at herself and laughs.

"Everyone has to go now. I know why but I don't really know why."

"I've thought that often . . . It seems a shame now that we've just met."

"You knew me before."

"I know, but you were quite different."

"Not so different."

"And so was I."

"And now?"

"Now we're not so different."

"Goodbye."

Lo feels a breath in his legs and he stretches off through the crowds joined by other crowds all heading across a stony plain to a forest. Above, bruise-coloured clouds get over-heavy and release torrents of rain. People are dashed to the ground while others walk on amused or saddened, or feeling blessed or lucky or pleased with their good judgement. Some of the battered sodden get to their feet and carry on, while others remain, clinging to the dirt, immobile.

The stones and weeds glitter.

In the woods people can be an arm's breadth away from one another without realising. Beech and oak and elm make up the forest, with pine interlopers planted and forgotten, ferny undergrowth and brackish streams that run clear in places where water tumbles down rocky beds. People crouch and sup. Shafting sunlight drops into the open where there is a clearing and some gather to talk.

Lo stands back to listen.

"In my house I have a chair next to the fireplace that's like the only place in the world. When I go to work I miss my kids and, for a moment, when I see them again at the end of the day, I miss them even more."

"Every night I would feel her hand on my forehead just before I fell asleep."

"I have a shed on my scrap of land and when I'm not digging or weeding, or what have you, or if it's raining fit to flood the world, I brew up and then I just sit there and look out at nothing in particular."

"The two of us going around the house at the end of the day, unplugging, closing windows, locking up; and then we meet, maybe, in the dark at the foot of the stairs; but I can still see her eyes, see. That's the best."

"We leave each other alone for the most part. It's better that way."

"I redecorate the bedroom every couple of years but always the same colours. We like it the way it is."

All the men sit: on rocks, on tree trunks, on grass, and some close their eyes the better to feel the sun on their faces.

Lo is one of these men.

An old one rises, exclaiming wordlessly. Among them in the clearing is a stag, stamping, snorting, turning—heat and a meaty odour rising around the beast; it thumps into the wood and after, at speed, cutting across and across each other come four hinds; and hard on them countless long-limbed, quicksilver hounds, heads raised or pressed to the lower foliage, yapping or silent. Lo watches their faces for smiles.

The crowd take to their feet and pass through the trees. Persistently now there is a beat and a *snap, snap, snap*—a *thrap, thrap, thrap*. The wood's edge is thickened with chesthigh brambles. Lo, and the others, push their way through, parting the sharp-spined boughs with their toughened hands, avoiding the springing rods that slash back at face height; clothes and skin are lashed or gripped, shins and backs and cheeks are striped with stinging lines.

Lo breaks out unmarked. There is a tower that is an axe, three mountains and a twitching hillock. The air is sweet with honey and bitter with iron. Crowds of men shuffle where they stand. A body flies up, howling, his clothes flake away and fall to the ground, the axe swings *chuh, chuh, chuh*; blood, viscera and shit spray the air; arms, legs and trunk dump onto different mountains and as they separate the penis and scrotum fly too and flop onto the hillock. The head drops onto a pile behind the mountains.

Another man loses his footing on the ground and the axe pivots and rolls, making the parts. The blade is doubleheaded, clean but not shiny, the shaft made from a single piece of wood. Lo imagines the tree from which it must have come, a cloud-reaching tree as old as dry land; a tree filled with sunlight, sap pulled from the lower earth, boughs and limbs that nodded, heart-shaped, serrated leaves that trembled while the trunk stood almost still in a high wind that crossed the plains from the early ocean.

The head thumps onto heads and another man rises into the sky. He calls for his mother. She doesn't answer.

Lo runs from man to man touching hands, shoulders—his mouth dry, unspeaking, his eyes asking and not finding. The ones become rising hundreds, thousands, tens of thousands, become parts, become rising mountains that settle and compress, finding an angle of repose. Lo turns to the forest but the bramble breaches have closed. No more men come through; the fields are emptying, the sky darkening. The axe swings and the ground drinks up the gore; froth floats on the earth.

The woman in the black apron appears in the sky, floating. She calls out, raises a hand and vanishes.

Lo is alone with one man who turns to shake his hand. Lo reaches. The man's heels are where his face was and the last of him is scattered.

Lo removes his boots; strips off. Rain falls and it is clean and warm. The axe stops moving and Lo dries in the new sun that appears over the mountains. Lo rises slowly and the axe cuts him and the limbs go to rest and his head falls onto the tallest peak and it coughs and spits and raises its voice and sings: "One day. One day I will be made whole."

Dick

DICK IS BURIED up to his belly on a cold shingle beach.
He has stripes shaved into his scalp, his beard hair. Dick
is roaring fit to best the sea. He is waving his arms in the
air, his hands cramped into claws, the fingernails cracked
and filthy. His manicure days are long gone.

Four men in long white wet shift dresses dance past,
holding hands, their arms stretched out like ropes, their
faces turned away from one another. The men circle
round, they return, they stop. The tide rips out to the
horizon in one instant, leaving mud gullies, sputtering
fish, bottles, nets, bones and turds (hard white turds) and,
further out, buoys and wrecks that creak and fall on their
sides unsupported by the lost body of water. Birds descend
to pick over stinking life. There is a distant maritime hush
and the sea is back in one motion. The dancers carry on.
They have seen nothing.

Dick says: "I have no use for a car here."

He laughs. He is full of words. They bubble out of his
mouth and dribble down his chin. There are tight soft
curls on his chest and back and shoulders. The skin is

yellow as good chicken fat, variously taut and puckered, a scattering of purple lesions that mean nothing, and scars, pink and silver trails, that mean trouble past—small and large injuries to others.

Dick says: "I outlived them all. My enemies, my friends." A cheap, white disc is in the sky. A sun that keeps all the heat to itself. Dick turns his head from side to side, nodding as if walking proudly up and down. He stops and looks to the front.

"Fear in the body outlives the body. How fragile and savage everything was. All the time I understood that I needed to survive. Time told. The world was different from what could be said about it, or all that could be known but not said. From all that hovered beyond knowing but could somehow be said.

"Talking was a kind of general panic. Back then. For instance: a young woman sat silent a few inches away from the gurning mouth of an older man who didn't quite look at her but spoke in a conceited bellow and looked terrifically pleased with himself. That is most of what I can remember about talking.

"Insistent desire and the nearness of death encouraged us to betray our friends, our lovers, our lovers' lovers. Me, at least."

Dick closes his eyes. Lying, star-shaped on the cold, spring mud, the sky an idea of blue. Dick smiles. Needles point in every direction from spindling branches of black thorn that cross above between eyes and sky. The tree

makes green for the first time but, somehow, doesn't gasp
or sigh or cry out. The wind swirls petals that drift around
Dick's body, not quite covering him. He closes his eyes
and opens his eyes and the shore is there again. The forever shore.

The four men walk past, their dresses wet. Three make
a windbreak and the fourth produces cigarettes from nowhere and leans to where one of them has made a lighter
appear. His thumb rolls the grinder, makes a spark, and
the wind picks up and takes the spark, and the one tries
again and makes a flame. The four stand around grinning, grimacing, tapping ash away from themselves. Dick
blinks the ash out of his eyes. The men smoke. The smoking is good, inconsequential. The cigarettes are over. The
men walk away.

Dick pouts his lower lip and spouts air to shift an ash
flake from the tip of his nose. He grunts. He growls. He
laughs. There is a silver shimmer over the middle of the
sea. Dick might be the only one to know that it will never
be exactly like this again.

"Eye-held toffee wrappers turned the sky yellow, pink,
green, a better blue, scented the air with caramel, crack-
led sweetly in hand; all gone except the colours that press
behind like the bruise of the world. All smiles. Drift on
that awhile . . ."

Wind eddies in circles then fails, dropping a little dust
some way off.

"Following the beautiful or ugly animal necessities,

pretence is how life comes about. Pretence shaped by the pretence of others, pressured by time like air weighing on a lake, or rock saddled on rock, or great, impermanent expanses of nothing grinding away on nothing. I told myself I had governance over the passing objects, some of them persons. I acted the part of a part that was necessary. I read enchantment in everything dead. How fresh and lovely is disbelief, flowering in the mind. I faked enlightenment. I made a flicker. What exactly? Mush in the head. Thinking, lighting.

"Today—this long, long today—I am needless. The wind in the cord grass is a constant breath, the grass anchors the sand, the shift and hiss persists but sand never flies higher than tit-height, saving my eyes from abrasion and yet my mouth is full of grit."

Dick spits. Where it lands it turns white stone amber. "The locality is known for the salubrity of the air . . . What this beach needs is children. My children, as they were. So I can be kind again. I will squat to their height and smile and tilt my head. And one smiles with fewer teeth than she had before she wasn't, while another dances around herself and sings. At the edge of sight, my boy, slouching, hands in pockets, dreaming. Big girl starts a story in the middle somewhere and I catch up with it by nodding and um-ing in the right places. Her eyes shine as she winds out the words; some she says for the first time. I can't help but laugh and, out of habit, cast my head around to check on the little one—still dancing, still singing. The boy looks over and grins. Together was always his favourite. We all loved 'together' then."

A cry comes from the air above and with it a hawk, scanning the dunes for careless life. There is much to be seen with keen predator eyes from its vantage: the friable coast, the estuary sweep, Dick on the beach, pieces of sea-smoothed glass submerged in the dry sand, yellow anemones, sea violets, bindweed, wrack; inland, a mount topped with a bandstand, a bowling green, a boating lake, a figure motionless by the river in black waders, black rubber overcoat and storm hat, rod rigid in his or her hands, three deckchairs part-buried in alluvial mud nearby, a fox floating, dead, in the water. Much to be seen but what the bird sees is not to be known.

"The question every time was: 'Where do I put my hands?' Touch was question and answer. Now it is the memory's wonder."

A darkness is on the horizon and another, nearer, in the air. The interwoven call-cry-call-cry-call-cry-cry of birds, their thousands of dirty white pinions falling and rising, battering the air, thumping past and past, the last few with a raggy flitter. There is a hissing, a rumbling, a bulking line of black advances from the sea at speed; it is the sea. Spume flies backwards from its leading edge, the mass moves beyond breaking. Dick's few remaining teeth shudder and click together as the beach shakes around him. He bows his bent arms in front of his face and closes his eyes. The torrent tide sweeps over throwing fist-sized rocks at his head and chest, one runs through his ear, tearing the cartilage. He is spattered with grit and silt. He opens his eyes. There is a weight of green water above and around him. Bubbles stream from his mouth and his nostrils. His chest feels crushed. There is a sting and retch in his nose and throat. The murk clears as the particles drift down. Near his head floats a man in a shift dress, his face panicked, the skin and flesh soft and leprous-looking. The body passes into the dark.

The sea falls suddenly in one piece. Dick draws air inwards, sobs and slobbers, coughs hoarsely, spits salt awhile—steadies. He blinks his eyes clear and looks into the near distance.

"You can't kill a bad thing."

One long in-breath and Dick closes his eyes and thinks in blurred time. His brain, he imagines, swells and hardens into a large salt crystal, cool and cloudy, its sharp edges scratching and scoring the inner bone. The memory of softness, of wetness, the memory of electricity, is lost. Dick's neck becomes sore from the unaccustomed weight. He tips his head gently forward and the rock rolls forward, thumping behind his eyes, which open. There is a screeching that could be gulls finding high unison, or a storm-ripped metal hull's final sundering, but it is Dick's own voice rising far outside his body and away. Salt is caked around his tearless eyes.

Dense clouds shift across the sky, parting, they halt and judder, and continue their progress out of sight. The sun appears directly above, too large, too perfectly yellow; it stains the world white. The air warms, the ground becomes hot; the sand changes colour from dark tan to dirty beige to milky mud, the smaller rock pools begin to seethe and bubble, the grass browns, frays and crinkles. The hair crisps on Dick's chest and arms, on the top of his head, on his face. Sweat washes down his body. Three men enter from the left, joined together at their arms, faces pointing away from each other, dancing elliptically, bending at the knees, swooning together as one. Flames start at a single hem and spread at once up the dress and across to another then another dress as the men scream. They keep in step, bending and swooning, circling, circling, until, mostly naked and hairless, they fall as one, a stack of charred sticks.

The sea returns fast and silent. The remains are washed away.

"I miss the night. Here there is only more light or less light. There are many qualities of gloom but there is always, behind even the dimmest sky, a solar insistency, the very thought of which makes my eyes sore. The greatest loss is that of the darkest nights, where one could see furthest, with the largest sense, the greatest contentment. On such nights the comforts of the dark were almost complete.

"I often went out among the people who made their living at night and spoke to them, laughed with them, paid them money for their saleable things. I was never the kind to take and not pay. There were stories everywhere. Stories in the body, stories in and out of time, stories in the chosen and the unchosen, stories under glass, stories under water, stories under flesh, hot and cold, stories in tumult and silence. I woke once, I don't know how, in a hotel room, a fierce sun outside held back by cheap orange curtains, sharing a small bed with an iron rope of a man and his broken wife: awake and staring at me with the same hungry smile. I did what I had to do to leave that room."

The clouds pull across and lower down, a grainy white-grey that traps a hovering light closer to the ground that makes time appear to hover too. The air has cooled and snow comes. The sea shuffles forward. Waves slump and fall apart, spreading towards Dick, stopping short at his belly.

"In the home she sat at a table near a broad white window, fitting together a jigsaw. She chose each piece delightedly and smiled as she pressed it into place. When she had finished the picture was complete but there were pieces left over. 'Dick . . .' she would say, 'Dick . . .'—and no more. Later she wheeled outside for a cigarette—the thick woollen stockings kept out the cold—and laughed at the nurses' jokes like she remembered what laughter was for.

"There I was, outside myself, looking at letting go, looking at what it looks like to be let go. My heart emptied, it was all out of time. The once-constant embrace of mind, of body, all that mother-holding, released without will. I feared that this had made her happy. I hoped that this had made her happy."

There is a dark bristling at the horizon. Moving rapidly, the fuss distinguishes itself into a jostling mass of boats, stubbornly rowed through the clashing surge and fall of the sea. Oarlocks glint in the sun. There are many people in the boats; cloaked and hooded, bare arms flash at each oar-pull. What might have been hours, in the world of hours, pass as Dick watches from the beach. For the first time today he can feel his lower body, every part that he knew but, most pleasurably, his toes, which he flickers. He pulls his feet up and, in the manner of climbing a ladder, steps up out of the packed sand, the broad stones, the sharp shingle and there he is, a whole body, a solitary, a standing man.

The boats ride up onto the shore. The forward riders jump out and through the broken waves, pull at the bows and run until the vessels find their out-of-water weight and must be dropped. The passengers scatter up the beach towards Dick, pulling down their hoods and calling out his name. He steps towards them, staggers on the stones, his legs grown weak in the ground, unfit for certain motion. He cries out. Here is everyone. Every face is known in love or rage or pity. He raises his arms to embrace . . . everyone. Tears pour down his face. A roar begins that might be laughter which carries from mouth to mouth. The sun swells above, giving all their share of light. Bodies bend and squat, arms swing low, there are taps and grates and each child, each man, each woman rises to their fullest height and smiles. Hands flash and twitch sending arcs through the air, a stone rain that batters knees and thighs, pelvis and belly, chest and shoulders, that punches eyes and nose, gashes chin and shatters cheekbone, bludgeons forehead.

The beach continues to fall as the sun withers and darkens. He tatters. Bone shows white, out of the wash of red, at shin and ribcage. The people pause and stand in silence before returning to their boats to push and pull out to sea. Dick has fallen to the ground. His day is over.

An Apple in the Library

THE LIBRARIAN SITS AT HER DESK. Unblinking, because unable to blink, unmoving, because unable to move. Air rushes between the stacks making a hoarse throat-music. The lamps are on and the ceiling is covered in scars. The books know but are still.

The reader pushes at the door, considers his choices when it resists him, then pulls on the door, which opens.

There is no knowing what the librarian is thinking. It is possible to know what the librarian is thinking.

The reader approaches her. "Do you have an apple?"

If it were possible she would be nodding, not talking, nodding, indicating the shelf behind the reader where the apple is. He turns around and turns back.

"I'm sorry. I need the apple. And you can't help me?"

The librarian stares at the reader. She knows that she cannot help. He smiles, considering his own simple appetence, it is a lovely thing, perhaps better than the apple sought; but still he must have the apple.

"Who brings you here? Are my questions cruel? I don't feel cruel although I know what it is. I can look at you and in seeing you not see you, only a dark part of myself which I do not recognise as myself but as you: the surface of you, made a thing; a thing I see and want, or don't want, to look at, to act on."

"Every day. Every single day," thinks the librarian. This is a loud thought but the reader cannot hear it. She thinks it again.

"Every single day."

"I'm sure the apple is near," says the reader.

"I have the idea of it in my hand. I possess the weight of the idea; not much, it is sufficient and, while lighter than many ideas, it is, at the moment, larger and more present than all those other thoughts."

"You are loud, unsheathed and boring, but you have a good smell: cleanliness with a superadded element, a bright unguent applied on the face with the fingers of each hand in a soft, swirling motion that awakes the skin, makes it live and feel like my skin, my flesh, once felt; a good smell; the odour of self-love, of care, of caring to be seen, of inhabiting one's aliveness and feeling it both never-ending and short-lived."

The lights blink off and the library stages a presentiment of endless darkness. The reader can smell the apple now; it is behind him or, perhaps, over his head, floating. He reaches up into the dark pursuing his sense and the lights blink on. He is staring at his hand reaching out to nothing.

The librarian has a thought but it is not in words. The reader wants to be guided to the apple by words, by the alphabet even, but the fruit is before, or outside of all that; it is possible that the apple leads to the words but not the other way round.

"I will look at the books. It's all right that I look at the books?"

The reader looks again into the librarian's face. "Everything I need to know today is in there. What do you do with it all, I wonder?"

"Love. It's enough."

"The apple is near and you are here and if I take the trouble to search I will find it."

"You are so vehement. It's right behind you; you might not find it; perhaps you will."

"I like being here with you; so little moving."

"Your lips are moving."

"Everything that I need is here and is unable to leave."

"Nobody talks like you; it's not credible; it's not a good thing."

"There's no resurrection except in small moments."

The reader turns and finds the apple. The apple finds his hand. The apple is more than one simple green, perfectly imperfect minor sphere, with spongy facets that can take the light and appear white in patches, but never completely. Wood, a stalk, and a tiny, heart-shaped, serrated leaf which, when lightly tugged, pulls back, belonging to the apple. He pushes the fruit into his mouth; his tongue's memory of other apples creates an unthought motion to test, to paint the smooth, cool surface. Between the head and the hand: the apple; and out of the head, the mouth, the teeth. The reader is biting and chewing and it all happens very quickly.

The librarian thinks:

"Is he eating the apple? Is the apple eating him?" The apple is finished.

The reader stands with one arm and hand free, the other bent slightly at the elbow, the core pinched lightly between his thumb and fore and index fingers.

"What I have had must come back to me: a thing, an event, done to, done by, me or who or her or him. The core turns brown, my fingers wet and sticky and fragrant."

"My eyes pour out meanings, longings—not for him— meanings that stop at my eyes, which are dry. Terribly dry." The reader raises the core to his mouth and his tongue works, the teeth click and snap, and white flesh pulses out and around the fibrous, seedy pith and the apple grows fuller and more itself, and a waxy, green ribbon peels out from the reader's mouth and spins around the fruit until it is complete. The reader places the apple back on the shelf. "Thank you."

The librarian blinks. The reader leaves.

Mareg

MAREG HAD BEGUN to think about comfort, about cosiness, but had put the thought out of mind.

Mareg left his room, a place of filth, in the first hotel in which he had stayed, in the country to which he had gone to learn about light; the light that he could not see at home. The room had been dark, cramped for him but spacious for the roaches with which he shared. Mosquitoes had hovered, selected, landed, fed; he pinched them one by one from his body and popped each with a thumbnail, spreading his blood against the wall above the greasy bedhead. There was a bloated, meaty odour of the recently dead rising in the warm air of the stairwell originating from platters, abandoned on the steps, of partially eaten, unidentifiable brown and yellow food that seethed with insects.

Mareg had hoped for arguments, singing, the cries of monkeys that might be men, anything to colour the night. He had come away to learn about colour, the colour he could not see at home, but had only begun to notice brown—brown and yellow.

Mareg was named Mark but he wanted, on self-announcing, to take longer to get to the end of his "who"—longer, but not too long. Mareg wanted to project unfamiliarity with himself to the people he met so that they could not approach the self he carried, his flyblown, yellowed, well-thumbed self. He wanted to hear a new voice come from his mouth. Wanted his body to stand without tremors, unsuperfluous, unknown in plain sight. Wanted to look into a blank page and follow the new mark, the opening scrawl. All of which is too much to expect from a new name.

The elevator was a narrow black cage, with one hard sliding door and another of compressible Xs, which rattled rapidly through the floors with a dopplered accompaniment of proximate, barely contained electricity. Stripes of yellow light passed up and down the moving room. The cage opened into darkness near a service exit. Mareg turned left and tried a door; light and smoke poured out and a maid sat there on a low, three-legged stool with her mules skinned off on the floor, legs crossed, facing away from the hand with the billowing cigarette as if it were a man she was ignoring.

"Sorry," she suggested. "Sorry," he said.

"Be sorry. Close the door."

Mareg closed the door and walked back past the elevator and into a hallway stepping over a large rectangle of jade-coloured tile that had slipped from the wall.

As he approached the desk Mareg walked into a drifting,

savoury scent. The receptionist smiled, white hair frizzy, protean, his navy blazer, capacious, brassy buttons, shining, tiny, half-moon glasses, flashing white. Mareg looked for the source of brightness and turned to find the sun sheeting in from outside. A black lacquer tray lay on the red leather of the desk, crowded with many small porcelain dishes; soup trembling at the frequency of the traffic, smoking strips of orange pork, a glistening vermicular heap of noodles, a wet pile of steamed spinach, spattered with garlic and dusted with white pepper.

Mareg had not come away to find delicious. There was delicious at home.

The receptionist nodded, smiled an indicating smile; a quarter-turn of the head was enough to take in a woman sitting on an armchair in the green shade of a palm tree, by a small table, awkwardly disposed near the entrance. She lifted her left hand and gave the forefingers a long slick of her tongue from root to tip before turning the page, scanning the page, licking her fingers and turning the page.

"She is beautiful but . . . I could never kiss a woman who does that."

Mareg realised that he had more of an accent than the old man and this made something important resettle in his mind which revealed that he had thought that certain voices implied limitations of mind and heart, and that, in this place, he alone possessed such a voice and a narrowness, a vitiated self, that was his and which he detested;

and that he could change only if he could exceed habits, voices, everything.

The receptionist stopped reading Mareg and ate. Mareg waited, growing hungry. More pages flicked behind him. A light, metallic collision echoed intestinally within the building. Mareg stared frankly at the appearance and embodiment of contentment that sat in front of him. This scene would give him something to aim for in the days ahead that, with luck, would not be lost in the arriving present, or some other more vivid moment of the returning past. There would be, he hoped, days of empty content.

The receptionist wiped his face with a radiant, white napkin and sat back smiling.

"Where do I eat here?"

"Don't eat here."

"I know that."

"Look, this is best for you . . ."

And the old man drew a tiny map, neatly, precisely, on the back of a business card. Mareg leaned forward and took the card and studied it, watching the black ink dry.

Mareg handed over the key and the bill was prepared. The amount was lower than he expected but he was alarmed to be informed that the hotel did not accept credit cards, which necessitated a fumble under his shirt for money. The greater the discretion he attempted, the more obvious the manoeuvre became until, finally, he undid the clips and pulled out a bulging, peach-coloured belt, trailing its straps. The receptionist's fingers flickered close to his breast pocket and Mareg turned to see the woman and a man, bright white sleeveless shirt, tattered hat and face-obscuring sunglasses, sitting up, alert, intent on everything except Mareg and his money.

He settled the bill and the receptionist spoke.

"You do know that you've lost the rest of your money now, don't you?"

"No . . . no, I don't. I mean . . ."

"Give the rest to me. Don't make the movement too big." Mareg did not hesitate and handed over the notes. "What shall I do now?"

"Leave. Go and have something to eat. Come back and I will return your money, less the cost of your meal."

Mareg knew his wallet was empty but looked anyway. He stood looking into the folds. The receptionist smiled at him and nodded for him to leave.

On the street the heat from the sun fell pure and white, breaking with silent force on every exposed or covered head. Mareg, separated into damp, heavy, moving parts, walked in the road holding the card, following the map— being a nuisance that needed to be avoided by bikes and scooters, cabs and buses, and shiny, long black limousines with darkened windows.

The map linked the hotel to the eating-place through four landmarks with the roads etched as lines, thin and straight, broken and elliptical, with no attempt at scale. The first mark was another, grander hotel outside of which a woman stood in a large white hat, wearing a long white dress; she would have been floating except that her feet were touching a scab of red carpet that covered the concrete platform in front of the reception's bright, revolving doors.

Twenty, or more, minutes later Mareg approached the Municipal Library, windows covered on the inside with curling brown paper. Steps strewn with sun-withered turds led up to double doors, their grubby brass handles tied together with a thick length of plasticised chain, joined in front with a massy padlock. A few steps away was a huge post office, not shown on the map. Men in loose blue shirts and baggy navy trousers sat on the wall outside smoking slowly, serenely, not talking.

Mareg walked a long stretch of narrow road crowded with thin, three-storey buildings, only standing, it seemed, with the support of their neighbours. Cast-iron balconies barely clung to rotten facades that, where the sunlight rested on them, glowed blue, pink and violet. On one side the row ended in wreckage through which weathered logs ran as props, bolted onto steel plates that rested on the ragged wall of the final house. Beyond this a great plaza, paved in blue stone, at the entrance of which stood two massive red pillars, devoid of decoration but scarred with chisel runs and hammer dinks and what might have been bullet marks. The words on the card read "golden palace" but there was no building in sight, no crowds gathered on the plaza. The people on the street were ignoring this wide-open space as Mareg was ignoring his own shadow. The last landmark was a sharp left-and-right turn away: a police station, an elegant steel and concrete building with narrow glass windows just over head-height on the ground floor. A tide of cool, sweet air poured over Mareg as he stepped past the entrance. After a short diagonal cut from the station he was in a square of tall apartment houses with shops and offices on the ground floor and a park in the centre concealed behind high hedges and tall trees. The café entrance was not obvious to begin with. Mareg walked twice past a storefront covered with a sweep of orange curtain, before turning and plunging in, right arm and shoulder first. Dust flew. There was a single step down that he could not have anticipated and his right foot and ankle twisted and, due to overcompensation, he began to fall to the left but was saved by a waiter who caught his elbow in a hard grip and strode him over to a small, round table in the corner.

The room was bursting with human sound. Every thing both inside and outside him pressed together, losing its distinctness, while, at the same time, seeming to fall apart into unrelated shapes that swam and scintillated, before disaggregating into what he could be sure was real, starting with a pulse of pain that came from his ankle.

Mareg looked again.

There were many tables, and lamps on every table, and people seated at every table, and a crowd of bowls at every table that steamed and hissed or stood silent: all fragrant. The waiter waited—a clean, white napkin hanging straight on his arm, his face clear of traces of emotion or intent. Mareg showed him the card and the waiter nodded and presented a menu in English. Mareg peered over the menu at the other diners and wondered if they had been given cards, perhaps with maps drawn on the back, but he thought that very few of them seemed like tourists and very many of them looked like regulars. Mareg described the dishes that he had seen the receptionist eat and the waiter listened, writing nothing down, and departed.

Over the neighbouring table loomed a man in a cream suit and maroon cravat, sitting in front of a small silver coffee pot and a bowl of blueberries, or similar, from which he ate in small, tossing mouthfuls. He poured the coffee, drank briefly and spoke.

"Everything you have heard about this country is true."

"I know very little . . ."

"That will always be true . . . I mean, that is the state of nature."

The man smiled. The coffee cup seemed a part of his hand as he raised it to his face and discreet again—itself—when set down in the saucer.

"I haven't liked this place until now," said Mareg. "I was in your country once on business . . ."

"You don't know where I'm from . . ."

"America . . . England . . . one of those . . . and I became very ill. The food was foul, the people ill-mannered, spilling disappointment wherever I went."

The waiter returned and stood close by Mareg, smelling of soap and sandalwood. He departed.

"I was taken to the emergency room of one of your public hospitals, I was in no position to protest, and I waited on a hard, yellow seat for a long time. An elderly looking, middle-aged man came in looking very distressed, perhaps drunk, complaining of a pain in his chest, although he was merely rubbing his ribcage as if soothing a bruise. He was pacific at first but within a few minutes he was on his feet shouting obscenities at the staff, the police, his daughter, against whom he pronounced an extended, and malevolent, sequence of detractions. A male nurse came in and remonstrated with the man who sat down grumbling.

"Shortly afterwards two scarcely dressed young women came in with a barely conscious young man between them holding himself—or being held—upright by resting, cruciform, on their shoulders. The women spotted the old man and immediately began to taunt him deploying a wide vocabulary of sexual suggestion. He ignored them at first, in a sullen way, but the girls increased the pitch and variety of their counsel and he began to shout that they were a disgrace and that he was old enough to be their grandfather. Eventually the old man stood, wavering, and said that if that was what they wanted, he would give them what they wanted; he unzipped his trousers, rooted about for a considerable time, provoking the girls to further gales of ribald laughter, until he produced from his pants a dirty, greenish, and mostly perished, old penis. The young man germinated into vigorous, protesting life, rushed across the room and punched the elder, shouting that he was a disgrace and old enough to be the girls' grandfather.

"The old man fell to his knees shouting. The women howled their friend's name. The nurse returned with two security guards who stood beside the elder, took an arm each and dragged him out of sight into the corridor. There was much shuffling and a wet thudding sound and the old man set up a high scream, like that of a burned child, and cried for help in words indistinguishable from one another.

"Some time later the automatic door hushed open and the old man crawled in, knees dragging, head lolloping forward, his face contorted and bloody. He gurgled and spat red onto the tiles. The nurse returned, pulled the man to his feet and spoke sternly to him, wagging a finger

and threatening him with more of what he had just en-
dured. 'But I came here for help,' he sobbed. The nurse
was implacable and the old man turned and staggered
out and it was only then that I noticed he was wearing
slippers."

Mareg felt discomfort at hearing this story but did not
feel accused, given that he could not see how he was, in
any way, representative of his nation. He thought that,
perhaps, his clothes or his shoes mutely, treacherously
evidenced his viciousness, or maybe even his hands.

He looked down at his hands and spoke.

"You met the people you don't meet at home."

"Yes, they were who I saw and that is what I know of
your country."

"It doesn't sound like my country . . . not all of it."

"Yours or thereabouts."

"You were taken care of?"

"I was not as ill as I had supposed and yet I was ill—very
ill. Once that was established I made a call and took a taxi
to a private hospital where no one talked and the food
was bland but fine. There was a brief procedure, which
my doctors here, later, confirmed was both necessary and
adequately performed, and I returned home a few days
later. This is what I know of your country."

"It's not what I know."

"Quite."

The man took a palmful of berries and threw them into his mouth. All the time the man was speaking Mareg had supposed that he was fat and only now noticed with surprise that he was not.

Both men began to speak at the same time, apologised, urged the other to go first and then the waiter returned with Mareg's food. People at the other tables began to smile and avert their eyes. The noise of each voice rose and came together in a mild, purposeful clamour. Mareg looked around for some way to feel less alone. His neighbour gazed directly, seriously at Mareg who stared down at his place setting and cutlery.

"You have ordered too much food. You have ordered a special meal, a celebration of exceptional good fortune. I am supposing that you are not, at present, a lucky man."

"It seems not."

The diners began to turn sympathetic faces to Mareg.

"I may as well eat."

Mareg picked up a fork and looked down at lush green, speckled red, glossy black, solar yellow and orange, immaculate white and pure grey; tasted the food heat, spice heat, salt and sour and sweet, the bright citrus, cinnamon, anise, clagging rice-fragrant rice, the meats, dense or soft or raggy, light and dark, the plump pink crescents of prawn, the smooth and heavy, light and fresh, dry and wet, sauces; the something hard and sharp, not for eating, which he rolled out of his mouth with his tongue; the slight bitter traces from the chefs' fingers. There was comfort and unfamiliarity and belonging and forgetting, a reordering of taste and memory, and the faint, happy agony of a dead fragment of self coming alive.

Mareg was filling up.

The waiter returned and placed a small, steel tray, on which rested the bill, at the edge of his table. Mareg placed the business card on top and hoped. The waiter pushed the tray gently back towards Mareg who looked up and, seeing nothing helpful, looked down at the empty bowls. The waiter crossed the room and in a double, left-and-right, sweep pulled the curtains open bringing in dust, leaves and a vast volume of painting, rippling, warming new light. A woman laughed and people began to rise, the feet of their seat legs grunting on the tiles, and each came over and placed coins or notes in the tray, to cover Mareg's bill, and left, waving and smiling.

Very soon the room was empty except for Mareg and his neighbour and the light that pulsed in from the street and beyond. The man stood, extended his hand to Mareg and said: "Welcome. My name is Mark."

Last Call for the Hated

CIGARETTE BUTTS WERE SCATTERED on the wet doorstep. Three or four more were inside on the doormat. Michael went to the kitchen and returned with a plastic bag wrapped around his hand, picked up the ends and folded them away.

Later he called his mother. "I'm fine love."

"Something's the matter, Ma. I can tell."

"You're such a good boy."

"You'd better tell me now."

"I wouldn't like to worry you."

Michael waited. The phone felt weightless, he might have been on his own.

"Well, I was getting on the bus today and a woman called me . . . an effing bee . . . A bitch."

She snapped at the word.

"A lovely lady, a total stranger called Mary, stood up for me and the horrible woman shut up then. I think it made her realise she'd no idea who else would be on the bus. The driver wouldn't lift a finger. I don't know why but this time it really upset me."

"You mean it's happened before?"

"Love, it happens twice, maybe three times, a year. I'm sorry to make a fuss."

"Don't. I mean it's not. I mean."

"Some people are like that. This one was rotten right through though. Face twisted up like a cat's knitting."

"Do you need me to come up and see you, Ma?"

"No love. I wouldn't want to put you out and anyway I've got Helen to look after me."

Michael agreed that he would see her on Saturday. He was going to the chip shop to get some supper before settling down to work. When he opened his front door he caught a sweet smell of mint and turned round to see long white streaks on the green door—the best part of a tube of toothpaste. He hadn't heard a thing.

As Michael walked down the street past the pollarded trees, people approaching him crossed over to the other side. In the chipper Andy served a woman before him, even though he was ahead of her in the queue. Or maybe she wasn't and it was a misunderstanding. She had the kids in the car and was in a hurry. Andy was doing her a favour. Michael was not in that kind of a rush, not at all.

Then Andy went to serve the man behind Michael. Definitely behind him in the queue. Tall, faded blue one-piece overall, floured in brick dust, spattered in paint.

"Excuse me, mate."

The man looked through him. "Hey, Andy! What am I? Invisible?"

"What are you having then?"

"Cod and chips. If that's not too much trouble."

Andy brisked his order together, slapped it on the counter, and took his money. He didn't even ask Michael if he wanted salt and vinegar. Michael hadn't realised until he was well down the road. He hated his chips without vinegar. Maybe there was some in the cupboard at home.

Michael had been made redundant—his role had been made redundant—in a restructure last year. The seniors hadn't really realised what he did, how much he did. They'd been in a hurry and hadn't got their legals straight. Michael hadn't rubbed their noses in it but they had given him a decent payout. Two weeks later the man who had replaced his old boss (junked in the same exercise) rang him up in a sweat.

"Mike, Mike . . . We kind of cut through an artery here."

"Are you offering me my old job back?"

"No, ah, no . . . But I'd really appreciate it if you'd help us. Help me out here. On a freelance basis."

"Contract work?"

"Yes."

"Then I'd like a contract. A written contract. That should be possible."

In the end he was back doing his old job, at the old rate, except this time he was invoicing for all the hours that they used to get for free, plus the odd latte here and there, plus he was working from home. The only thing he'd lost was the job security but that had turned out to be a rope that was tied to itself.

Michael was happier out of the office anyway. The few people who, when he started, had glinted briefly in a friendly way were tinfoil, not silver. His own tiny hope for amity had been reflected back at him just the once. It was easy to mistake that kind of thing for kindness.

With the extra money Michael had bought a car. He used to ride a bicycle everywhere but after a succession of thefts he had given up and started to take the bus. There was always aggravation on the bus, especially in the summer. He tried not to think about it. Except that one time, when a perfectly normal old man looked him hard in the face before spitting—spouting—on his shoes. The man hadn't said a word. Maybe Michael had been talking too loudly on his mobile, but everybody did, and that was an extreme reaction. Wasn't it? Michael had called him a dirty bugger and a couple of lairy men had stepped up out of nowhere to tell him to leave it out. He backed away with his palms out and it had gone no further.

Inside on the doormat was a fresh pile of rose-tipped cigarette stubs. He cleaned them up. The phone rang once, twice. He answered. There was no one there. He hung up. The phone rang again, once. He answered.

"Who is it?"

There was a crackle, or it could have been a cough, but he couldn't hear any breathing. "Listen. I'm hanging up now," and he did.

The phone rang again and he pulled the jack from the wall. He didn't know why he kept a landline anyway.

Michael put the fish and chips on a plate, got the ketchup out of the fridge. There was an inch of ancient red wine vinegar in the cupboard.

"I should throw it away, really," he said, and then stood surprised at the sound of his own voice.

The computer woke up and music streamed to the speakers in the living room. Good music that Michael had chosen because it was soothing but not narcotic.

There was a loud dull bang upstairs. Michael forked a bunch of chips into his mouth and went to the spare room at the front of the house where he saw a slick, juicy circle on the window. For a moment he thought it was on the inside. He approached. There was no one in the street, but in the pocket garden he saw the remains of a burst peach. The window cleaner was due on Thursday. It wasn't long to wait.

Michael went back to his supper, which was cold, and he ate it, chips first, then the fish.

There was nothing in the weekend that he spent at his mother's. His sister Helen showed him her notebooks. She was trying to write a book, or something. Michael couldn't see why she would want to tell her stories.

"That's really good, Helen. It happens just like that," he said.

"Thanks," said Helen, "I know it's not very good."

On the way up someone had razored the back of his rucksack and stolen his player. Michael liked the old tech. Helen had noticed when he slung his pack in the boot. He was sorry to lose the headphones, which were high quality, bought in Frankfurt when he was working on a project over there. His mother had wanted to buy him a replacement. She always wanted to make it all better and every single time, for a shard of a second, he still thought that she could. "Let me do it. This one small thing. Let me," she pleaded.

"Let me do it. This one small thing."

"That's very kind, Ma, but no. I've plenty of money. It's no trouble. I wish I hadn't mentioned it."

As he left on Sunday to catch the two o'clock train she took his warm hand in her two cold ones and he had a twenty in his palm. Michael crumpled the note and rested it in a pot plant in the hall where it looked in place, like a withered flower.

The standard carriages were packed out. A family had spread out into his reserved seat. As he walked down the aisle he formulated the words in his mind, asking them politely to vacate his seat and let him sit down. But, at the last moment, he thought better of making a show of himself. He pulled the reservation ticket out without their noticing, placed it in his pocket, and moved on. Michael paid the surcharge to travel first class instead, it wasn't much after all, and he settled into the empty carriage with his free newspaper and complimentary tea and coffee. One cup of each so that he'd had his money's worth.

The train travelled through quiet places with unused piles of gravel, abandoned cars, hard patch farms, grey and blue, grey and yellow, grey and green warehouses— or they may have been factories. He must have seen twenty, thirty playgrounds and not a single child playing in the mild sunshine. Michael paid close attention to the gradual aggregation of the city, trying to discover the point at which nowhere became somewhere.

Out of the barriers and on the way home, he took another train, a bus. On the pavement near home was a rosy puddle frothed with scum, the smell of bleach. Michael spoke to himself: "The butcher stays open by supplying local restaurants. Only the elderly buy their meat here now, and they are fewer every day."

He stepped past the shops and headed for the footbridge over the dual carriageway.

Fear grabbed him immediately—he is three, he is eight, he is fourteen again—a gang of boys, men if they want to be, hoods up, swaggering along. There was no way of passing them without triggering an offence, an excuse. The traffic bullets by fifty feet below. He's always thought those open side panels on the walkway were a danger. You could slip through, be sucked through, be pushed through and then fall, fall, fall, before breaking on the ground to be mauled by cars, trucks, vans, cars.

The one to watch out for is the short guy. The others

are actors; he is real. Michael looks at how his eyes are moving, what they see, what they don't see. Maybe they're missing him.

Michael tries the left-hand side, walks steadily but not too fast. The little man tracks over to him. Michael keeps going. He's found a line of sight, an object, a dirty flag in someone's garden, somewhere far beyond where he is at this moment. He feels the texture of the path beneath his shoes. The gang is a few paces away. Michael is there, making contact, still in motion; the little man fixes him, he returns the stare—he can't help it—and the man says:

"All right? Are you all right?"

Michael nods, mumbles, and the boys blur past.

Michael walked down his street; the lawns had grown greener since Friday. His pack felt lighter. Home was in sight.

The gate was open. There was a dent in the hood of his car and on the side a long key scratch. A couple of hundred to fix, that's all. The magnolia stellata had come alive in the garden, its great purple-stained petals exclaiming upwards, the bin knocked over, the recycling boxes scattered around. Michael was halfway down the short path when he caught the scent. He released the deadlocks, turned the Yale and, pushing slowly, opened the door. On the mat was a heavy load of excrement, more cigarette butts, many spent matches, and from the smell and the stain, petrol.

Michael put on a pair of heavy gloves and got to work

setting everything straight in the garden. He piled all the refuse onto the mat and dragged it out into the street, into the middle of the road. He pulled out a box of kitchen matches, struck one and let it fall to the mat, which flamed up blue-yellow-orange.

"That's the way to do it," said Michael.

He watched for a while. No one came out of their houses. Michael returned and cleaned the inside of the door. Momentarily he considered cutting out the spoiled area of the hall carpet with a craft knife but instead took an old towel from under the sink, damped it, and laid it down. He opened the windows. It did not take long to clear the air.

From his bedroom window he could see the mat still burning. The sun was going down and no one was about. Michael imagined he could hear the flickering but he could not. He opened the soiled mail wearing rubber gloves. Mail shots, bills, a letter from his girlfriend in New York, an envelope marked with a dark scrawl made illegible by filth. Michael couldn't imagine why she didn't just email him as usual. And then, he could imagine it—imagine exactly why. "Dear Michael—From this distance I can't know why I was ever involved with you. I can only think I was punishing myself for . . ."

And so she went on about herself, not knowing that she'd dropped her news from a height of four thousand miles only to be buried in shit.

Michael put down the letter and picked up the other sheet, a square of yellow paper folded in half. He had disposed of the crapulous envelope it had come in but had not yet read the note. Michael read the words and looked up to find he was staring at his reflection in the shower room mirror.

"You. You are hated."

He went into the bathroom, found the plug with its broken chain, leaned into the bath to press it in, and set the hot water leaping free. In his home office Michael started up his computer, placed her letter in the bin and pinned the yellow note to the noticeboard. On his Hotmail account he brought up her email address.

"Darling, I understand. Believe me, I really understand Love (if I may), Michael."

In the bath he read the same page of a book over and over until the water turned cold, and then he went to bed.

The sleep seemed to go on forever, he was deep inside it, not dreaming exactly, but aware that he was asleep and when he woke he felt an infant calm in being there. A clean, white light saturated everything, a cool breeze played around the room. He pulled the quilt up to his chin, turned over and went back to sleep. Some time later he found himself awake, stood up, stretched, and went in to check his email. He had a reply from her that he deleted without reading. He read the yellow note for a while. Then he sent an email to work telling them he was taking a holiday.

On returning to his bedroom from the shower he saw something outside in the street. Pressing close to the window he saw the mat burning, the flames roaring orange. Head high.

In the kitchen Michael switched on the radio, moved the dial around without finding anything to listen to before turning it off. He slowly made breakfast and ate, staring softly at the new blossom on next door's apple trees. The sight kept renewing itself until time overtook vision, or vision time, at which point Michael wasn't even looking.

He cleaned the house thoroughly, pulled every plug, switched off every socket, secured every window. He emptied the food from the fridge, the freezer, and the cupboards into three black bin liners, tied them up with their own excess, carried them to the end of the garden and threw the bags, one at a time, over the fence and into the park beyond.

Michael placed his suitcase on the back seat and stepped into the car. He got out and ran into the house, upstairs to his office, reached over his desk to the notice-board and unpinned the yellow note before barreling down the stairs and out into the street. Michael put on some music before pulling away, making sure to avoid the fire. He was just turning out at the end of the road when another vehicle sped past scarcely missing him. Through a dirty back windscreen Michael could see an arm shoot up, hand open in apology. The car lost its hold, skittered left and right at the rear before powering off. Michael turned right and drove past the park. The mock-Tudor bandstand was ablaze, the flames rolling slowly, wetly into the sky. A large gathering of birds, of different species, watched on the grass from a safe distance.

Michael drove the car down the ramp onto the Circular Road and accelerated across the empty lanes. Fifty minutes later he was nearly at the airport, and was yet to see another person, when a large silver motorbike surged, almost silently, into view in his mirrors. The bike pulled in front, slowed to a steady glide, and the driver waved a leather-gloved hand, which Michael took to mean "follow me." This he might have done but the bike took off at an uncatchable speed.

In front of the terminal building was a toy box scattering of vehicles, many with their doors open, headlights on, indicators clacking on and off. Michael stopped, retrieved his luggage, and walked in over the fragments of the automated door. The silver bike was lying on the ground next to a ticket machine. All the check-ins were closed but he could see the flashing heels of someone running through the premium-class gateway and he followed.

There were no security guards, no customs officers or police officers. Michael passed through a detector and the alarm sounded but no one came. Airside the travellators were still working and he walked along looking out at the blank sky, and the runways congested with planes and service vehicles. Turning from one terminal spur into another Michael heard a low, avionic hum and walked more quickly, jogged for a few paces before thinking better of it and slowing to a comfortable stroll. As soon as he saw the lights he smelled brewing coffee and bakery goods. At the counter were two airline representatives, a woman and a man, navy smart, radiating solar smiles.

"Good morning, sir."

"Good morning."

"May we?"

"Oh, yes," said Michael giving them his passport. They ignored it. He patted his pockets as a way of thinking about what he needed to do next and pulled out the yellow note. "Thank you. Please come through. We are just completing boarding."

The man offered his hand and took Michael's bag, and they walked together down a ramp to the plane.

"How do you like your coffee, sir?"

"Black and big. Please."

"Certainly. Sugar?"

"No, thanks. And a blueberry muffin?"

"Yes. For you, sir."

At the entrance to the plane, gathered in the cramped space near the service area, the flight crew, sunny, wide-eyed, greeted Michael, wished him a pleasant journey. He turned left down the aisle and passed through a curtain.

All eyes looked up from what they were doing. The passengers made a long intake of breath and released it in a great, outrushing sigh. Michael smiled and in return everyone smiled back.

Elsewhere

THROUGH THE PLASTER and brick the clear-eyed boy stands, impermeable in the stream of time. The room beyond is clean and uncluttered. A large painting hangs on one wall, an unfigured pattern in brackenish tones of purple and brown. Tea rose is faintly on the air. A woman sits on a comfortable sofa. She barks. And barks again. Short, dry sobs, torn up from a place inside where everything that was alive has compacted into a single hard point.

The boy blinks.

Outside: the road, the path, the strand, the sea. No one visits in the winter and the residents could walk the sand unimpeded by pleasure seekers from other places. Except they do not walk. The winds are harsh and searching. It is either raining or about to rain. Everyone here feels porous, but no one talks about it. The sky is a vast anvil hovering over the sea.

The boy belonged to the sea. He would walk the winter beach. Dig tunnels in the hard wet sand until his hands were blue-red and numb, and stung when he put them in the fleecy pockets of his jacket. Further up the head the boy would sit for hours on the grassy dunes that overlook the stone beach, watching the procession and recession of the tides. The small hawks buffeting in the high air, scanning the world for life. A mile away a broad, half-buried sewage pipe dumps its slick load into the sea, just about half a mile too close to the shore, and when the seasons rise and the wind turns, the stink rolls over the land.

The boy watched closely for the first warm day when he could go to the Drop to swim before the old men arrived. Ragged ribbons of deep green seaweed border the natural pool, said to be fifty foot deep. There is a worn-in run-up track, but the boy preferred to climb to an awkward ledge several feet higher and, from a standing start, cartwheel into the air before cutting, cormorant-style, straight into the still-cold water, making as little sound as he could. The long wait, falling and rising in the darkness, a perfection of movement; all the stale air of winter expelled in huge, pearly bubbles, then breaking, surfacing with a long inspiration that felt like new life beginning.

The half-term holiday starts today. A small number of families will come for a cheap break bringing their strollers, picture books and waterproofs. The house next door is a holiday cottage, uncared for and uninhabited most of the year, even in high season. A few minutes ago a minicab pulled up, its exhaust rattling on the tarmac. Two children, a boy and a girl, perhaps twelve and nine, jumped out. The parents and the driver chatted unhurriedly before unloading, exchanging payment and giving thanks. The taxi shuddered off and the four stood in silence. A curtain flickered. "Let's get the keys," said the mother, clutching a letter. "Can I press the buttons?" asked the girl, and the mother read out the combination to the key safe. The door open, they worked together to get their belongings inside.

The woman rises from the sofa and heads for the kitchen, slippers whispering across the carpet. She starts to make tea without wanting tea. She paces up and down as the kettle makes a small tidal roar. Sitting down she gazes, unseeing, at the picture on the gallery mug: a landscape with a giant heading into the distance. The boy appears, running, stops in a blur, turns and stands waveringly still behind the wall facing her. He lifts his arm and waves to her slowly. Once, twice. They stare directly, indirectly at each other, missing one another, as they did in life.

She talks.

"Tea is better when it's sweet. Tea is one sip after another until it's all gone."

She empties the dishwasher putting each item away in its proper place, rinses the mug and places it in the machine's upper rack. She returns to the hall, a grey lump lies on the floor, the late-delivered newspaper. She returns to the sofa and begins to read. There is a story on the front page about a government minister who claimed money on his expenses which he was, strictly speaking, entitled to under the rules but which, in today's more straitened climate, seems an excessive amount of money. But, as it turns out, he is withdrawing his claim. There is a story about a member of an international aid agency who has been kidnapped together with an Italian journalist. A video of them reading prepared statements is on the web, a screen still of which is on the page. "We are being treated well," they say. There are stories about football, an actress and her new film, a report about foods that might be unhealthy that most people, even doctors, think of as healthy. There is a colour banner to encourage you to read the supplements that come with the main newspaper. A picture of a yacht floating on a bright blue sea. There are no people on board. Maybe it could be you on board. If circumstances changed.

The woman opens the paper with great care, folding the left-hand page tightly against the back page. She reads page two with great concentration. The boy walks slowly into view behind the fireplace. The flames blossom out from his feet and rise to just above his knees. Page two is finished and she moves on to page three. An advertisement for sofas but there is no need for a new sofa in this house. Next are the murder pages: rage, greed and the pitiless pursuit of pleasure. The boy presses forward but makes no progress, his hand and arm move as if to wave again, but he does not. The woman reads on, turning the pages and carefully making them flat with her hands. There is more news from around the world, mostly places she has never been and to which she will never go. Not because of money or fear but because there is no need. Many more unnecessaries fill the following pages. It is not clear which are the adverts and which the features. There are many pages about different sports. She reads them all.

The boy is gone.

Upstairs in a large, light-filled room, a man sits at a piano. He plays fluently, decisively, his back upright, head nodding, feet pumping the pedals. The lid is closed. He stops. The boy appears behind the wall facing him. The playing begins again, the same piece, taken a little faster. The boy recognises the music. He has heard it many times. He hears it when he is alone, but only the first twelve bars repeated over and over. The man's fingers press and stab at the shiny, black wood. They are white and bruised. The boy looks down into his face; it is grey, misshapen, stained with exhaustion. The boy is searching for someone. Himself. The man stops again, his face wet with tears, he takes a clean, white handkerchief out of his blazer pocket and dries himself. He lifts the lid, pauses for a moment, and begins to play.

The boy leaves.

He goes to a room with no windows, no doors, no furniture; a bare concrete floor, a single, white light bulb. He lies down on the floor and tries to sleep. There is a book he remembers in which a boy and a girl, a brother and sister, go wandering, and time loses them. It is a comedy. They meet the dogs of time, which are big and fierce, their bristly snouts snuff up mortal trails, the scent drives them mad but they cannot leave us alone. The dogs are toothless but their breath turns the living into dust. The boy and girl escape. They have adventures with timeless creatures like and unlike themselves. They tell each other jokes and stories and sing songs. And they travel beyond forever, and never return.

The family next door appear on the pavement all rugged-up against the last of the winter storms that is moving in from the west. They are talking comfortably, laughing often. Even the youngest is not daunted by the prospect of an icy soaking. "Let's go down to the sea!" she shouts. "Shush a bit sweetie. Now." Her father presses a stud closed at the neck of his coat. "The sea it is." And they promenade across the road, down the path to the strand and the sea. On the beach they build a great castle, like the one they visited on holiday in Spain, in a year when they had more money. They settle on a tartan rug and eat a home-made picnic. Rain clouds curdle darkly above. The children run off alone to look for shells and seaweed, and other drifting treasures with which to decorate the castle, while their parents bring out a flask of tea and a secret supply of chocolate. Just for the two of them.

The wind rises, picking up the sand, drifting it over the Spanish castle. The man and woman stop talking and pull closer to each other. The children are gone, poking about in rock pools and caves, probably. The wind stiffens, moving on the storm, pulling back the corrugated clouds to reveal a depthless blue sky and the first sun of the infant season. They close their eyes to enjoy the new warmth, rock back their heads, ignoring the not-too-distant cries or screams, grateful that it is raining elsewhere.

Remains of the Dead World

THE WILD, grey fields stretch out to the horizon, punctuated by smoking moraines of rubble. Furless creatures scramble, four-legged, near the mounds searching for prompts and relics. Close to a brake of trees rusty green petals turn on a windmill that stands in the well-ordered garden of a solitary house. On the doorstep sits a skinny, smiling girl with a shotgun on her lap. Older, male voices sing out from the rooms behind her. A scant mile away in a dark declivity at the heart of a wood sits a naked old man outside a canvas tent. On a rotten stump in front of him stands a large crow. "Dada's gone. The leaving started with him spending more and more time in the shed; making I suppose. I had a toy once that he made me. Made the same one for my sister. And my brother. And my other brother. It was a lorry, a wooden one; it smelt of glue. The wheels were wood too but I don't know how he made them. They looked like little chocolate biscuits. Carra hit the babysitter in the face with his—the front bit—he fell right over. And then he didn't get up again. Dada burned it then—the lorry. Might have burned mine."

The shadows curdle around the base of the trees. The

old man stares at his feet. The crow looks on at everything, closes its eyes. The man leans forward and whispers:

"The crow wears my daddy's dentures. I'd recognise that smile anywhere. His filthy beak opens in the dark and I can see those yellow gnashers sliding around in there. Well, you wouldn't expect them to fit properly now. I didn't know crows could get cold, only I found out when I heard the teeth chattering. To be honest, I find it much easier to understand what he's saying when the teeth are out, but he won't listen to me."

"Shut up, you mad old fool. Can't you let an old crow have his bit of a kip?"

"You yourself. You've got the manners of a . . . raven . . ."

"OUT!"

"I'm sorry. I'm sorry. I'm sorry . . . I'm really sorry."

The old man begins to sing softly to the crow to soothe his hurt feelings. A song about the moon rising over the old canal with the prams and bicycles and the chemical drums jagging up, and a large, hairless doll, floating pink on the oily water. A beautiful song.

"You've a lovely voice, old man."

"Couldn't you call me by my name after all this time?" says Dada.

Pink light slides down the side of the house. The girl smiles on. Then stops.

"Mamm found Dada asleep under the big bay. The one all tangled with brambles. The berries could have fallen into his mouth when he was asleep. He'd have had a funny dream then maybe. One about a big house with a floppy, peachy hat instead of a roof. Much nicer than our house. Or just nice I suppose.

"Then he began disappearing altogether. Out to the fields back there where he'd sleep in the mud under the cross posts. Mamm said the fresh air'd do him good. Do us all good. Just after that I had to leave school and Dada moved on to the old wood. I never liked that wood when I was little 'cos I thought it was full of wolves and cows at night-time, and in the day when you went walking, it had burnt mattresses and vodka bottles and plungy needles and it smelled of wee. The big boys'd ride their nasty mopeds around and around and bring those big, muscly babykiller dogs there for their runabout. But then the crow arrived and the bad boys went away for ever."

The old man looks into his lap.

"My hands, they're not shapely, but they're big. Like fleshy gloves placed over my proper hands. The kids liked to look at them when they were little but as they got older they began to be scared. That made me sad, when I thought about it, but it wasn't long before they stopped being afraid and became—instead—indifferent. They're just hands after all."

He poked the dead fire with a length of railing. There hasn't been rain for weeks but it's still cold.

"A fire would be good," says the crow.

"One more thing I didn't learn how to do," says Dada.

"The boys didn't like Dada living in the wood and one night they ambushed him at his humpy and beat him with sticks. He cuffed a couple of them but the others held him down and poured petrol on his face and hair. They were about to strike their matches when the crow appeared. I'd never thought about crows before and I still don't know what I think really. They're beautiful aren't they? So dark and perfect with eyes that flash silver when they blink, but my old teacher, Mr Finker, said they're crawling with fleas and lice, just like foxes but not so stinky. Mamm told us that the crow took a great breath and blew the twitching little fires of the matches out, and then he breathed again, deeper that time, and blew the boys up into the air and out of the world, their mopeds following them, twisting in the big, black sky."

"I was gone a long time," says the crow, "and when I returned the forest had shrunk to little more than a large copse. The earth was slathered over with a hard crust of black and grey. The rivers had been captured and buried underground. The smell of all was sour and thin and it caught at the back of my throat. The world had been the wood—my wood—and now it was nearly gone. The savages who had done this lived unhappily in their dirty boxes, making the real world wretched with their point-less contraptions."

"I knew it. I said it," says Dada, "the walls, the wheels, the glittering rags . . . all the voices emptying out and filling up and emptying out again. Nothing was ever still . . ."

"Nothing ever is still."

"As you say," says Dada, bowing his head.

"We're still here in our bit of a house. Carra helped Dada dig a well where the crow showed him—and a poo pit too. Dada said it's cleaner in the woods, and 'all walls fall down some time,' and 'you wouldn't want to be standing under that big load of dusty muck when it comes to earth.' But Mamm won't hear of it. She worked hard for this house, and that's where she's going to stay, especially now that the mortgage doesn't count. The others live on the plain in holes in the ground and once in a while a tribe of them come up here looking for food or clean water. We give them a little of what they want for, but if they come after dark I fire off at them. That's my job 'cos I'm the best shot."

"When the crow cast those bad boys out, he found he had his breath back and then . . ."

"Whose story is this?" asks the crow.

"Everybody's?" says Dada.

"No. This is my story. You just have to live in it. I took to the skies above the great city from where I could see many patches of sterile green, large and small. One nearby had a hill encrusted with a large white building, on top of which was a tall needle . . ."

"Aerial," says Dada.

"I alighted on the aerial and soon my mind filled with what was to be done. I fell asleep again but this time only for a few days and when I awoke I pulled back my wings, filling my chest with the smoky air, I closed my eyes and blew as hard as I could and for seventy days and seventy nights my breath raged over the dead world; the roads, the buildings, the spoiled dirt, the screaming wires; and the named, the nameless, counted and uncounted profusion of things, things, things, that had been hacked and hauled from the earth's body and were everywhere clagging and messing and masking its beautiful skin. And all that was left of the dead was dust and fragments and a single house. Yours, old man."

"Not mine any more, crow. And why don't you say more about the people? What happened to the people?"

"Who? There are people left. More than enough. Don't think about it."

The crow sniffs and walks about the stump, flitters his wings briefly, and settles.

"Nim, my big little brother, goes out digging in the mounds. I know he does 'cos he hides the things he finds in his room. And I know that 'cos I search Nim's room when he's out digging. Figgett, my little little brother, found me snooping yesterday but I know he won't dob me in. I didn't scare him. He just knows who's his friend. In a box on top of Nim's cupboard I found a bag of chocolates, I tried one and it was all dry and gluey, and didn't taste of anything. I had to spit it out but I kept coming back to the bag for a great big sniff. Lovely.

"There was a small, white computer that wasn't broken, but it didn't work—like all the rest—and there was a black block of a camera with film in it and everything, but what's the point of that? Mostly what I found were lots of bits and pieces which helped me work out what Nim is really looking for: a bicycle. We've got the wreck of a scooter out the back and a little bike that would suit a circus midget but I reckon he wants a real, grown up bike."

The dusk is coming on and the woods begin to twitch with hungry, curious life.

"I didn't want to be right, crow."

"You weren't right, old man. What you thought you knew was nothing: a coincidence. Just lights in your head."

"I keep thinking. If only I'd taken my medication, the world would still be here."

"You did nothing and the world is more here than it was before. The trees are rising and soon the great wood will return."

"And what happens then?"

"The seasons go on for ever and ever until the sun dies."

The old man waited for a moment.

"Not much to look forward to. Is it?"

The sun blazes lonely in the sky and the girl stands in the garden with her back to the light.

"I've got my backpack, some food, water bottles and the last of my shells. Nim came back yesterday wheeling two bicycles. They were too big to hide and, anyway, he was too excited. Now we can go away across the plain, away from the trees and then we can be sure that it's all gone. That there's no more of us left. That there's no more than what remains."

How to Read a Picture Book

FROM A RED OAK a large branch sweeps to the forest floor and a fat squirrel lumbers off drawing heavily on a zeppelin cigar. Twitching his mouth to the left he releases a long grey cloud which breaks up into shapes that form letters saying the word: "sorry." The gathering of children, formerly quiet—hands folded in front of them as instructed, hair bunched, braided, brushed, noses wiped, tummies full—bursts into screaming applause (except the two facing the wrong way).

"Hi. I'm Sorry the Squirrel. Of course, that's just my creative name. My real name is Maximilian Liebowitz, but you wouldn't be able to pronounce that now, would you kiddies?"

"No!" they shout.

"Yes!" cries one bespectacled boy in front. "What's your name, son?" says the squirrel.

"Philip Liebowitz."

"Hey! Maybe we're related . . . although that would be a genetic impossibility. What most people don't seem to realise is that I'm not a midget in a suit. I'm a real squirrel. Although sometimes on a beautiful summer's day like this I think it might be nice just to slip the fur off for a while and cool down. But I can tell you kids I've seen a skinned squirrel and it's not a pretty sight.

"When my agent first suggested the name 'Sorry the Squirrel' I said: 'Sorry?' I laughed for a whole week. I love that joke and I'll always use it on a fresh audience. Today, at the kind invitation of Coram Summer Camps, I'm going to talk to you little darlings about how to read a picture book. You might think you know all about it but I'm here to tell you to think again."

Sorry takes a long sizzling drag and jets out the words: "THE WORDS."

"I should have started with pictures really, because pictures are just like the world. Aren't they? A picture of an orange means an orange. A picture of an elephant means an elephant. Although it could be an elephant that stands on two feet and if he's wearing a silk purple dressing gown it only seems natural that he'll have a little conversation in him. Words are just mute smudges until you know what they mean, and when you put them together they can tell all manner of things. There's plenty you can't say with words. You can fall through words down into a seething belly world of billions of objects and notions, all shrieking or hiding. And then you might read a simple story, go out to the park to play and when you come back all those words have come to mean something else entirely.

"Anybody here scared of words?"

A few hands fly up with a large number resisting, red-faced, their damp hands pressed to their knees.

"Give me a scary word!"

"Crocodile," says a tiny girl in a green dress. "Well, you look like a crocodile little one."

"Give me an unscary word!"

"Ice cream," says Philip. "Two words." Sorry winks.

"I ate the ice-cream crocodile with my shiny silver spoon . . ." All the children cheer, except for Philip.

"See. You can make scary things funny or silly or good. Or good things scary. The giant witch turned me into pistachio ice cream and gobbled me all up."

Sorry runs up and down making the kids scream and laugh by pretending to be a hungry witch-giant. He stops and everyone soon settles down.

"Sometimes when Mommy or Daddy are very tired they'll stumble over the words. Say them in the wrong order. Miss a page or two. Fall asleep drooling so that you have to shake them awake and, if you're lucky, they'll start over from where they left off and, if not, they'll say: 'Look Max. I have to make supper and clean the kitchen and write a report for work. So I can't go on reading. Sorry.'

"The words tell you who is in the story and what they do or what happens to them. Noriko, a little girl, and her teddy bear Boz, meet a monster called Fizz who's very scared of teddy bears. When Fizz discovers that teddy bears don't have big claws and bad breath and mad, staring eyes, but are lovely and cuddly and help you get back to sleep when you wake in the middle of the night scared and lonely and crying, he decides that he wants a teddy bear of his own. Boz, having said nothing in the story so far, pipes up and tells Noriko and Fizz that teddy bears all come from the Teddy Bear Mountain many miles away through the forest."

Sorry stops and the children lean forward. "So that's some of what words do in a story."

Several children put their hands up and they mutter like a crowd. Sorry points at a girl wearing a pink beret.

"What is it?"

"Mr Sorry, my name is Cynthia. What happened next?"

"Noriko, Boz and Fizz went to the Teddy Bear Mountain, having lots of adventures on the way. Fizz found his very own teddy bear to hold and love forever. The End."

"What happened then?" asks Philip.

"Fizz grew up and discovered that he wasn't a monster but a boy just like you, and eventually he forgot all about his teddy bear and it languished in a cardboard box in a dusty attic until he grew up and had a child of his own. He sent the bear to the cleaners and gave it to his son, but he never played with it because it looked so old and weird. The End. The Double End.

"Sometimes there are two stories being told at the same time. One for you—about a dog who's a genius and a spy who foils an international conspiracy to close down the local butcher and replace it with a whole foods superstore. One for your worn down, weary, cynical old parents—about a lazy, good-for-nothing fleabag of a dog who for no reason at all bites a hippy outside the stinky old butchers that no one goes to any more."

A few sapling hands wave in the air.

"Cynical is when you don't believe that anything can be good any more, except maybe your kids. Between the time of your beautiful incomprehension and the moment that you finally lose the will to see goodness you'll be able to see both stories and find the two of them funny. That's probably the best of life."

Sorry pauses for a while. The children remain quiet looking into the still black pools of the squirrel's eyes. High above the trees a lark sings its pure song in flight.

"Birds." Sorry spits. "Birds always got to ruin the peace." He takes a smoke and balloons it into the air above him: "PICTURES."

"Pictures show you what the world is like or could be like. Or they show you the strange stuff that's inside your head—I guess words can do that too. The world is nothing like pictures really. It's not flat and you can reach out and touch it and it touches you back sometimes. I'm told that making pictures can tell you who you are, but you have to draw. Anybody can draw. One of the stupidest things that grown-ups do is to stop drawing. The last year I did art at school I got three per cent in my final assessment. The teacher said there were too many blank spaces. That's when I stopped drawing."

Sorry twists and curls his tail and makes a rolling shuffle

dance with his feet that raises some dust.

"Three skinny mice skitter across a red-tiled floor pursued by a rollingly fat woman in a dirty apron waving a vast, bloody knife. See how they run? Straight into the wainscot. Bunk! Bunk! Bunk! Blind, you see. The woman harvests their tails with one sweep of the knife and drops them, still writhing, into a jar with six googling eyes. The mice shivering with shock crawl along the board until they find a hole where they squeak into the darkness. Did you ever see such a thing in your life?"

"NO! NO!" yell the children.

Sorry steps forward to give a handkerchief to Cynthia who is crying.

"This was in a book I had when I was young. It terrified me but I had to keep going back to see whether it had changed or not. But pictures don't change once they're made. They're like everything else you do in your life. Once you act you're done. I can pretend to tear up the words as they come out of my mouth. I can spend years perfecting my forgetfulness. I can destroy the evidence. But it doesn't work. Pictures you can slash or burn, but they're still something you made. Beware kids. Be careful what you make." Sorry places the cigar between his teeth and grins, turns around and runs up the trunk of the tree directly behind him. Halfway up he hits a heart carved into the bark, flips, twists in mid-air and lands on his feet in front of the audience. Sorry coughs heavily while applause spatters around him.

"Grown-ups can't help hiding stuff. Even if you live the

same day every day new things get thrown on top of the junk you already have in there." Sorry taps his head with his cigar finger. A little hair is singed sending a slight odor of panic wafting through the air.

"The memory of ice cream is always overwhelmed by the experience of ice cream. Anybody here like ice cream?"

"Yeah!" cries everyone except Philip. Sorry looks down at him.

"No?"

"I'm . . . I'm lactose intolerant."

"Every one can have a little something later. On me," says Sorry.

Sorry runs back behind the trees for a quick pee. He strides out slowly, talking.

"Then there are all those things that are right in front of you that you don't recognise. Things or ideas or feelings that you can't fit into what you know or maybe you're distracted or sleepy. Hey! Can you see the bird in that tree? You can't see it? It's there. I'll tell you about it so you know, then there's a chance that you'll be able to see it too. It's a bird in that tree: greenish-grey with whitish-grey stripes on its wings and a short, sharp seed-cracking beak."

Sorry gestures towards a scrubby pine in the near distance.

"I see it! I see it!" a few of the kids yell, and the bird flies away.

"Then there's all of the stuff that people hide

deliberately. Bad things. Mean things. You've got to find out about that for yourself. Sometimes people practise concealment simply for their own amusement. They hide things for fun. For instance, my Uncle Manny lived in the same apartment for twenty years and then he met a lady—a squirrel that is—and they married and, of course, they wanted to renovate. When Auntie Becca stripped the wallpaper over the mantelpiece she found the words: 'Your life is a pathetic sham.' Auntie Becca put a frame around it before she painted the wall. It's still there.

"Now with picture books part of the fun is looking for the hidden stuff. Take the picture of the wolf and Red Riding Hood stalking silently towards the woodcutter's cottage. Now turn it upside down. In the scattering of golden leaves at the bottom you can just make out the words: 'Tidy your room.' Then how about that book *Tiger Night* where the baby tiger can't sleep and the daddy tiger has to keep reading him stories until they both fall asleep at the end. Now, if you take the first letter of each line and put them together it spells: 'SAMSAMCALLME-PLEASE.' On the last page there's the picture of the tigers asleep on the sofa in the living room and on the wall there's a mirror and in it you can just make out a telephone number."

Sorry takes the cigar out of his mouth and examines the wet, black tip before returning it for a long, slow pull. A mist of smoke fills the air over his head that becomes: "TIME."

"When you're reading a picture book you can ask yourself the question: 'How much time has it got in it?' In *Crazy Lily and the Birthday Surprise* all the action takes place in the thirty seconds after Lily fails to get the present that she was expecting. In *Ulysses* all the events in present time take place over a single day. But that one doesn't have any pictures. In *Amos and Boris* months go by as the mouse sails his home-made boat out into the ocean, hours pass as he floats in the swell slowly drowning. He's rescued by the whale in an instant and their friendship endures for years. The book takes only ten minutes to read but it has all this time packed inside, and when you remember reading it that time returns to you adding to your own small portion. Reading can slow time to a drip, drip, or push it on in a rushing, sinewy torrent like a snow-fed river in spring. Books let you circle around time, find the root of time, lose time, recover time. People will tell you that reading—especially stories—is a waste of time. Don't believe them for a second."

Sorry coughs out a "C" that stands on the air for a few seconds. He hacks again and nothing appears. He turns back to the children.

"People say to me 'You're a character' and I say 'How do you know?' For characters it's the pictures that tell you the most. Look in their faces. Happy, sad, naughty, kind, deranged, demented, depressed. Personally, I don't wear clothes and I'm always amazed by how a simple change of apparel transforms the way people read each other. A simple suit will make the whole complex hinterland of a person disappear. A faded, yellow summer dress makes the weight of bitter experience float away into the sunshine leaving behind whatever you're able to hang on a smile. And I won't start on hats and hair.

"Then there's action. Characters can do what you expect—the witch turning her children from good to bad with a wave of her wand—or least expect—the little girl with freckles and pigtails lifting up a police officer with one hand and throwing him across the room. To make a story you can write a list of characters—rabbit, bishop, soldier, baker, loner, miner, stoner—and a list of actions—sobbing, shooting, scratching, smiling, stealing, sliding, soothing."

"Do they all have to begin with S?"

"No, Cynthia. They don't all have to begin with S . . . Put the verbs on the left and the nouns on the right and read them off together any which way to get your picture. Scratching rabbit, sobbing soldier . . . You try."

"Smiling miner," says a lemon-faced boy wearing a woollen hat.

"Excellent. Now you've got your picture you can start asking 'why?' and keep going until you've got a story.

"One thing that you get a lot of in real life, but not in picture books, is inexplicable action. That includes situations where you just don't know the answer, but you might find out eventually, and those occasions when the answer seems too small to fit the action. For instance, when your neighbor's smashing up your car with a shovel because your dog peed on his gate."

The children giggle.

"You can keep on asking but sometimes you never get to the why."

Sorry makes a guppy face and puffs out "PERSPEC-TIVE," blows once sharply and the smoke rearranges as "POINT OF VIEW."

"Who's telling the story? Is one person telling the picture part of the story and another telling the words part? In *Mitch's Riches* a little boy called Mitch tells the story of his life of wealth and privilege. The fine clothes, the best sneakers, the coolest hair, the newest cell phone and, his prize possession, a vintage Gibson guitar. Mitch pities his less fortunate friends but recognises the non-material pleasures of their lives and, in any case, is open handed to a fault, showering them with candy, the latest games consoles and tickets for all the big ball games. The pictures show Mitch living in a half-derelict house in a wretched neighbourhood, his clothes are threadbare, his shoes split, his mother is sick and uninsured, and his father is long gone. Mitch walks every day to the nearest subway station and plays his four-stringed toy guitar for the commuters who smile and throw pennies, but never quarters. One day a professor at the big music school downtown is out at the end of the line visiting his loser brother and he sees Mitch playing. He recognises his enormous musical ability and before he knows it Mitch is uptown living the high life. Never happens, right? Mitch sticks it for a couple of weeks then goes back to the slum and his perfect dream life."

Sorry takes a deep breath and blows out of his nostrils. "SETTING" floats faintly in the air.

"Setting just means the place where the story happens. It can be everyday like the park, the playground or in the kitchen with mom. Or it can be fantastical and familiar like a cozy burrow with an open fire, chintzy chairs and a giant stuffed carrot over the mantelpiece. Or your own house after dark with tiny goblins sitting around an open fire they've set in the middle of the kitchen table, where they're tearing up and tossing in your homework, laughing as the fire roars up to scorch the ceiling with a green flame. Or it can be totally new and crazy like a giant purple dome in the polar wastes of a chocolate planet where androids lounge in hot pools of vanilla milk while humans rush around doing their bidding.

"Often you'll find the same story in different settings— the child who can't sleep reappearing as a bear, a fox, a bird; in caves, sets, nests or dens. Changing the setting is often part of the story—as with Mitch. In real life settings can change when things go wrong like your dad loses his job and your parents fight and then separate, and you have to choose who you want to move in with, and you choose dad but mom gets angry and takes it to court, and you have to move in with her, and she never forgives you and now you're living in a poky apartment, but that's all right really except your new school sucks, and none of your old friends will cross town to see you. So, yeah, things can change with the setting."

Sorry pulls one more time on the cigar, walks back and stubs it out in the middle of the carved heart. He blows in the air and a faint, unreadable mist appears momentarily. "Endings. Endings in picture books are there to tell you that everything ends—even you. The beauty awakes, the wolf dies, the hobgoblin gets his hat back, the prodigal rabbit returns to his mama's warm embrace, the men in white arrive with great, big nets to take the squirrel away. In picture books you can have a second ending after the first one, like in *Fox and Cox* where, after a desperate, muddy chase, the fox escapes by chewing a hole at the bottom of the page. The master of the hunt, Mr Cox, a turbulent pack of hounds, and a score of scarlet-coated hunters on huge chestnut horses run out past the recto margin. But on the endpapers you see all the former adversaries, plus a rabbit, a hare, a grouse and a partridge, seated at a banquet in a great hall all roaring and rolling and throwing food around."

Three men dressed in white carrying huge nets run out into the clearing. Sorry runs to the nearest tree shrinking as he goes. He leaps, light as a leaf, and disappears into the foliage. Philip stands up and the men brush past him.

He walks out of the park, puts a cigarette into his mouth and then takes it out again, reaches for a hat that isn't there, and puts the spare hand in his pocket. Standing still on the sidewalk Philip can feel the green behind him. The traffic rumbles slowly down the avenue, bright horns prick the rush, and the day carries on past its end.

Play

"PLAY IS NOT FUN. It is what we must do in order to live. If I win I might live well before I die but, nonetheless, I experience the anguish of playing the game. Anxiety is the primary condition of play. Our smiles are grimaces. Our laughter: the sound of rage surging up from our guts."

His glasses slid down the bridge of his nose. He pushed them up with his index finger. His glasses slid down the bridge of his nose.

"Most of you people are the product of a mentality that sees idleness as the enemy of material progress. From the earliest age you were enrolled in Mandarin classes, oboe classes, ballet, extra math, extra, extra math. Even sport was not permitted to take place without tuition, direction, coaching, drilling and controlled diets. Those with more enlightened parents, who realised something of the value of leisure, scheduled your play between specific hours to gain the maximum return from the time and effort invested. Ironically, while they were depriving you of play, your parents themselves were engaged in a free-ranging and highly charged game of position, gain and, for all I know, parental love. In promoting your needs, their needs, their part in the game was promoted above your needs thereby, ultimately, and with the greatest compassion and efficacy, teaching you about the real nature of play and inducting you into the game.

"There will be one or two savants in the room with idiot, or savage, parents who gave you no encouragement, and provided no resources to help you on the path to knowledge and achievement. Nevertheless here you are. Well done. The terrible hunger, the crippling sense of disadvantage and the burgeoning, almost rageful, sense of entitlementthat you feel will propel you forward into wisdom. You may resist but you will be a player.

"Alain LeLond describes the bourgeoisie as 'the ludic class.' This is catchy but dumb. There are class conventions about being seen to play and among the proletariat this is associated with inauthenticity, but the reality is that everyone is in the game. Even suicide is a move; as young people you will have your own much-admired examples. Counter-formations are positional plays, some sincere, many reducible to *épater des parents* or 'thumbing one's nose' at those who you will, almost certainly, succeed. They exist primarily to facilitate sexual relations between the young and to animate marketing campaigns. One of the main reasons why the young are often unable to look into the future is the necessity to avoid despair brought on by the certitude that one is a type, with typical behaviour and a typical end. The end, that is, before the end."

"Scott. Look man—he's got egg on his tie. Like egg yolk in a phlegmy dribble down his front."

"Do you think he has anyone in his life that will tell him if he's about to venture into the world soiled? Obviously soiled?"

Lena pushed forward between Scott and Sameh from the row behind.

"He lives alone."

"Balls blown off in Korea," said Scott.

"Wife died in a tragic hunting accident," said Sameh.

"A sexual anhedonic," said Scott.

"A toxic halitotic," said Sameh.

"Evidently," replied Scott.

"He's divorced with one son, remarried but they don't live together. His son Daniel is in prison, accessory to murder—involved in receiving stolen paintings. There was a kerfuffle and someone died."

"Kerfuffle?" said Scott.

"What don't you know?" said Sameh.

"I research everyone," said Lena.

Scott laughed briefly.

"This is where I protest innocence at some outland-ish—and wholly fictional—misdemeanour that I now presume Lena to know about in order to raise a laugh."

"Please don't," said Sameh.

"Quite," said Lena.

The professor looked up and blinked, fumbled a square object out of his jacket, opened the square, his wallet, and stared inside before returning it to his pocket.

"Today, however, I don't wish to talk about the contemporary game but, what I'm at the moment calling 'pure play.'

"Play is dementing. Being in play pushes us to the edge of our skin. On the surface we feel a spectral itching that spreads and jumps, stops, starts, evades the usually efficient scratching of our close-bitten nails. What nervous pressure in one's back or neck causes one to lose grip, to feel a bloody knot in a wasted bicep, to wake up aware of our left hand as claw, boiling red or rotted grey or shining, leather yellow? We are so interested, so heightened in our absorption, so alert and yet distracted from the object of interest by the very intensity of our interest. When this desire falls back we become disoriented, perhaps depressed, but we see more and play better, or at least more successfully. Are we having fun? I am not having fun."

He took off his tie, balled it up and threw it in the wastepaper basket. "His feet look like two loaves of cheap brown bread," said Scott.

"Oh sweet bread—that in the darkness of the wrap— clings one slice to another—never meeting—filled but unfulfilled . . ." started Sameh.

"Shut up," said Lena.

"When were you invited?" asked Sameh.

"For the time being Scott and I are doing the 'Scott and Sameh' thing."

"With a latent post-adolescent sexual thing for added luster," added Scott.

"With no sexual what-he-said," said Sameh.

"Exactly," said Scott.

"The rule is you only interrupt him if you have something more interesting to say than what he's saying," said Lena.

"You've just broken your own rule," said Sameh.

"Play starts as freedom. Our eyes, clear and precious, drink in the everything, our brains shape-sort: the swirl, the mess, with our inherited portion, against and through our tiny experience. We push against the little materials of our infant world with our warm, damp hands. Some things move away, others stay still, still others push back. We can fall off a table holding a pomegranate and crack our head from side to side and the ruby jewels will spread across the terracotta tile, but our mind will be safe after a short recovery. The sunlight shadows the garden fence, the leaves hiss softly in the breeze, the check blanket warm under your back. The world is playing with you, freely.

"Agony seethes in your jaw; terrible growths are forcing their way out and up. There is no understanding that this intense suffering won't be your permanent state of existence. You run into every corner of the world, reaching, climbing, falling, seeking out father to bite in the neck, the knuckle, mother to bite in the neck, the nipple, playmates to bite anywhere. Then after some months you have teeth—a full set of teeth. The smile is yours. Beautiful, dreamy and sinister. You are no longer free."

He turned to the whiteboard, picked up a pen and began to write in tiny blue letters. There was a low hush as the students leaned forward to scrutinise the marks. A hubbub arose as reading glasses were changed for stronger glasses.

"I looked at those words after class and they don't make any sense," said Scott.

"Doesn't he always lock the room? How did you get back in?" asked Lena.

"I didn't. I hid and then climbed out the window and onto the fire escape before drop-falling to safety with the grace and empty purpose of a cat."

"Liar . . . Probably," said Lena.

"I took notes," said Scott.

A loud sequence of marker squeaks made them turn to the front but there was nothing new happening so they came back to one another.

"Let me see," said Sameh.

Scott reached into a satchel and produced the number 3 notebook in which he faithfully copied everything he didn't understand and Sameh held out his hand to receive it.

"I'm disappointed in you Scott. This is Coptic script."

Scott chewed his lip.

"What does it mean?" said Lena.

"It means: 'You can read this but can you read . . .' then it's just gibberish as far as I can tell. Or it's a code written in the same lettering."

"He's taunting us," said Scott.

"He doesn't care about us," said Lena. "He's playing with himself."

"I will work on the assumption that he is giving us the questions, and the answers in outline, for the end of year exams and see where that takes me," said Sameh.

Scott turned around and stared at him with an intent, animal vigor.

"I will, of course, share," said Sameh.

"Secrecy is integral to play. I move the colored beads, separating out the shapes, making piles on the floor. I talk to myself all the while in a low, sibilant murmur. My brother walks in. 'No!' I shout. He picks up the red and white threading lace and drops it in the bead bucket before leaving. No one knows what I am playing even when I tell them, by accident or on purpose, that the game is called 'olives.'

"The presence of the hidden, the facticity of secrecy, is often given to be interesting in itself—the concealment containing nothing but a fibrous pith around which the fruit of the game has swelled. But on occasion—rarely— there is a secret that has a real weight and radiance, that signifies, that designs a world around itself, acting through people and things indifferent to their well-being. The voice of the secret could be mute, or ubiquitous and imperceptible, as long as it remains largely unknown. I give no examples."

He walked across and across the platform. The students stared down from the terraces and through the security screen—a blemish-free wall of glass that separated the teacher from the taught. He stopped and ground his heel into the floor, with his hands in his pockets, before looking up searchingly.

"I can no longer recall the secret of the game that I called 'olives.'

"Pichard argues in his 1955 book *Play in Play* that the objective of all play is the abolition of biological reality. I parse the words and gain their sense but I don't really know what they mean. What I do know is that for most people, for most times, the fundamental basis of biological reality has been, and continues to be, pain—physical and emotional pain. A couple of hands of Pinochle won't distance the suffering caused by a detached patella, the sound of your father's voice saying over and over in your head 'We never wanted you. You were a mistake.' Or even a simple sudden loss of faith. We have two options at this stage in our race's technological development: drugs and courage."

"Death," said Lena. "He forgot about death."

"Death is generally available but I tend to see it as more of an abdication than a solution."

"He can hear us?" Lena whispered. "Up here?"

"Evidently," said Scott.

"But he wears a hearing aid," said Sameh.

"I imagine that is why he can hear us. There's a clue in the name," said Scott.

"Paradoxically Pichard stresses the essentially embodied nature of play. On investigation this turns out to mean nothing more than that one needs a body in order to be able to play. It is the kind of dressed-up statement of the obvious that is represented as an intellectual breakthrough but is, in fact, a banal utterance with no analytical power whatsoever."

He stopped and swept the loose hair back over the top of his warm head and looked on, blinking, at the slight reflection of himself in the glass.

"There is real work to be done on the relationship between body, mind and play but this has hardly been possible until recently. You will have already read de Waal's work on primates. Please read it again.

"All play is imaginative, that is it tends toward the realisation of a self that is larger, more real, more fully formed than the tight knot of stunted desires that are our originating selves; that dense fire that so readily dies before we do.

"From out of the drifts appeared a group of boys—aged 9, 10, 11—each holding and shaping their portions of snow. A little one peered at me from beneath his hat grinning, his head tilted to one side like a bird's. My face broke. 'He's smiling! He's smiling!' yelled the scout and they hurled their snowballs—mostly missing.

"What is happening inside the enlargement of spirits brought about by pure play? It is more than just a mood. It is the creation of a real environment for living, out of all the intangible materials without and within us, real and unreal. Without play we are homeless. I'm not saying that play necessarily generates a happy home, merely a home—a place where we can live alive. Children, quite frankly and determinedly, include others of their kind by excluding them from play, or including them in the role of the tormented. This is sometimes misunderstood as scapegoating but is, in fact, a technique for bringing life to life by bringing the dead and the despised to the edge of the playing group saying: 'Look what it is to be unhappy, unalive, we . . . we who are radiant and right.'"

"Is he telling us a story?" asked Scott.

"Yes, and it's your story. I can see you as a cheeky lookout," said Sameh.

"Turn around boys so you can see me raise my eyebrows querulously," said Lena.

"Uh. No," said Scott.

"I'm going to go back through my notes and collate all the passages that sound more like a story than a lecture. I'll leave the pages overnight and read them again in the morning. If the text behaves like a story I'll submit it to a magazine."

"I never see you taking notes," said Sameh.

"I'm the universal auditor. I'm always taking notes. I can wake in the morning and write a complete transcription of my dreams if I wish. Which I don't because dreams aren't important."

"I agree. Your dreams are not important," said Lena.

"The Kiutl nation, who used to govern this region before it became a wilderness, developed a festival of transgression in which they would engage in their traditional games and contests but, for a few days, players were expected to cheat in the most creative manner in order to carry off the prize. The most devious and innovative, perhaps even the most wicked, would be presented with a black-feather cape and welcomed into the elder group—whatever their age. This eventually evolved into a permanent system of values whereby the elders were permitted, even required, to break the most sacred laws of the people at any time that they wished. This gave the people of the rule a clear and true understanding of the purpose of piety and the limitations of rightful conduct. The Kiutl lament became their central cultural achievement: a song of bitter rage at the unfairness of a society where rule-players were constrained in a world of arbitrary disadvantage and loss ending in an afterlife where they would remain forever seated in cold silence on the stone benches of the Hall of the Righteous while the elders passed on to a paradise called Iutl or 'Confusion.'

The last Kiutli died of gasoline poisoning in 1922."

"I took this course last year," said Scott, "and everything's changed—the lectures, the reading list, the term papers—all except the title."

"This is the seventeenth year that he's run the play module and it changes every year," said Lena.

"Which I knew," said Scott.

"Have you heard that he writes most of the papers that he cites?" said Sameh.

"Which I didn't knew," said Scott.

"He pseudonymously dialogues with himself reserving his most scything vituperation for authors who are, in fact, him," said Sameh.

"I didn't know that," said Lena, paling.

"What did you say?" said Scott curving his arm, cupping his ear and wiggling his little finger.

"At least I know what I don't know," said Lena. "That's what you think . . ."

"You disgust me."

"I disgust myself. You should try it some time." Sameh yawned.

"Getting to the truth, determining what's right, has been and gone. Overpowering is all there is just like before and er . . . Well, you know the rest. Look outside now."

Twists of trunks and boughs writhed in a wind that no one inside could hear. Leaves shook and surged. Every green moment was never before and never would be again. Dry knots of unfinished fruit rained down staining the terracotta pathways with black streaks. A lone student ran to take cover in a rustic shelter but she switched direction and made for the dorms. Still some distance from the ivied doorway she changed course again and picked up speed making for the lecture theater but, as she moved out into the open onto the wide green lawn, the wind picked the woman up by her feet and shook and turned her through the air. She landed heavily and plunged her fingers into the warm turf in an attempt to anchor herself but the wind gathered behind her slight body and rolled her out of sight.

"We should go out and help her?" said Sameh.

"The lecture's not over," said Scott.

"I know Bobbie. She'll be back," said Lena.

"I didn't see anything flying through the air that could hurt her. She didn't take off or anything." Scott laughed. "I don't know why she couldn't keep her footing."

"The blunt hands of the northern air push aside the unwilling, the unsteady," said Sameh.

The professor opened his briefcase and took out a cell phone. At first he seemed uncertain as to how to turn it on but soon he was talking.

"Bobbie in the wind," he says. "I think she's OK you just have to stop her from moving any further. Call me back when she's safe."

He turned to the class.

"I wake up and nothing is within reach. Time, my glasses, my wife. I have no need of notes but a shower and breakfast are essential and by the time I reach the campus all the conditions are set fair for a good lecture. I hope that you agree."

Everyone nodded and said "yes, yes" and then the professor's phone rang: big bass drums and a distant squall of feedback. He looked surprised, grabbed the phone and answered.

"Yes, of course. Thank you, Roger.

"Bobbie is fine and back in her room. All of you say 'thank you' to Roger the next time you see him."

The students muttered their assent.

"The distance between people is organised through play with the whole spectrum of reality and unreality becoming actualised. In contrast the world of incapable play, incompetent play, dictated or compliant play is one that is only minimally alive. The person is somatically operative but the spaces inside and around them are congealing perhaps already set solid. They cannot move toward themselves or others. Play is impossible and civilisation is at an end.

"Daniel reached out toward the panda bear, reaching to find it: the bear's eyes, two toffee-colored discs of plastic, dead but kind, alive with the kindness of its creator; the kindness too of Daniel's mother. He seemed to reach out forever, his hand turning to show a livid, misshapen thumbnail. Jean came no closer but her smile grew bigger and bigger. Daniel fell toward it but still came no closer to the bear. The guard was hit once. He had been someone once. He was hit once and then he died. The painting—a triptych—was recovered six months later. Now everyone can see again the painter before exile in his tuxedo, looking out, smoking, not asking for help. Just looking."

"I told you that Bobbie would be all right," said Lena.

"I'm glad that Roger is there to take care of us," said Sameh, "when we can't take care of ourselves."

"So am I," said Scott.

Outside traffic signs were uprooted, green waves of cold water washed over the lawns, dark, arm-like branches fell from the sky. In the lecture theatre it was only comfortably warm but the professor took off his jacket, folded it in half and threw it on the floor. He picked it up, dusted it off and put it back on.

"The facts of any case were always believed to be unknowable by the Kiutl, so six members of the defendant's extended family were required to consider a question that could not be answered. The first one nodded and nodded until his head slid off his neck and rolled into his lap. He then carried it across the courtyard and placed the head in a rush basket where it began to talk. The next five lost their heads in the same manner as they too could not answer the question, and soon the air was filled with crying, singing, declaiming, whispering, barking and moaning that came from the basket, while the six torsos sat on the trial bench twitching, their hands rolling, feet tapping.

The judge settled his rotting wig and proceeded to the basket where he squatted on his haunches and listened to the testimony. He stood up, breaking wind with brassy vigor before returning slowly to the judicial throne.

"The verdict was guilty. The family torsos ran toward the basket, bumping and trampling one another as they went, they plunged their hands in to search for their heads. They kneeled together stroking hair, feeling noses and ears, avoiding the mouths for fear of biting and eventually each found his head.

"The defendant was taken in a penitential walk to the centre of the courtyard. Each step accompanied with blows from a ceremonial stick marked with symbols that illustrated his crime and administered by his own, youngest child. He knelt in the dust and apologised to the twelve corners of the world. The girl ran with the stick and threw it into the furnace where it quickly flamed and crumbled at which point the crime had ended.

"Daniel answered fully all the questions that were put to him. None of the other guilty were available so Daniel took all the blame upon himself, despite the fact that he did not strike the blow or have any intention to injure or even was present at the robbery. Nonetheless, he had selected the gallery and the painting and found the buyer—unnamed in court. Daniel accepted that without him the guard would still be alive, or perhaps dead but in his own way, and therefore it was right that he took this death upon himself."

"The night students will come soon but they won't be able to see the stars for the clouds," said Sameh.

"Does he give another lecture then?" Scott asked Lena.

"He shadows the course but I think it's all different. The night students gather in the lounge theatre, there are fewer of them, they sit and drink coffee and eat cake. Maybe they talk about their jobs and their children."

"You don't know do you?" said Scott.

"No," said Lena.

"To begin with the external world appears to us magically—instantaneously. We wish and some version of that wish happens eventually, or not at all, or imperfectly. The wish-wait becomes a permanent feature of how we relate to the world even in the most impulsive, active and driven people. In play the new person experiments with not-waiting and discovers action and response. Through this we learn that there is no magic but, naturally, we retain an enduring magic sense and the belief that we can urge satiety out of nothing. We have an expectation of intervention and we can either wait for the event to be made or we can move toward hope with guile and energy. This motion makes play happen or perhaps it's essentially what play is. Very early on the responses to the initial play motion—the reaching out—are often caused by the child itself. This is well observed in the lone child but is just as great a feature of those who are alone in company—the disregarded, the inward looking, the rejecting. Objects are seized, animated and brought into repeated combinations of conflict and harmony with one another. This could well be happening internally with language, as awkward new sounds are rolled against each other, rattled, scraped and squeezed to make meaning happen—to make meaning join up with all manner of things inside and outside.

"When the police knocked on the door the senator answered wearing a white tuxedo. The servants had been let go early. He led the officers up the central staircase and down a cream-carpeted corridor talking easily all the while about the snow emergency, complimenting the service in general terms on their professionalism under duress. The officers remained silent. SDS Thomas Whiteacre had unclipped his firearm holster and rested a gloved hand close by on his belt. They entered a suite, passed through a room with a 24-hour news channel playing opposite an empty two-seater sofa. Through an open steel door they were ushered into a large beech-lined room that was empty except for a red leather bench and a three-panelled painting.

"'I found this in my house,' said the senator. 'I returned from my office and I found this painting here. It doesn't belong here. I thought I'd call you before contacting the museum.'

"'With respect senator,' said Whiteacre, 'you didn't call us. We are here on information received regarding a stolen painting.'

"'And that's it,' said the uniform pointing and grinning.

"The senator gave the officers times and dates, the cleaner who had called the police was questioned and later deported, and no charges were pressed against the senator or any member of his household. That is how I imagine it taking place."

Sameh stopped taking notes.

"If only the seats were comfortable then I would feel completely at home here," he said.

"The bathrooms are squalid," said Lena.

"I would never use the bathrooms here," said Sameh. Scott turned around awkwardly and looked at Lena. "Would you like to . . . I mean . . . go for coffee after this is over?" said Scott.

"Everywhere is closed now," said Lena.

"Sorry. I only . . ."

"Which means we'll have to go to yours," said Lena.

"Yours," said Sameh.

"Mine," said Lena.

"Great!" said Scott and a little squeak escaped from the back of his throat.

"The journey from magic to reality, from inchoate self to individual, inasmuch as that ever happens, is mirrored in the therapeutic journey from sickness to well-being—inasmuch as that ever happens. In all cases that distance is travelled through play. Play is the place where transition happens and how it happens. All the students as they leave the theater rise up like birds, because they are birds, and flock like birds, because they are birds, and wheel and cry in the dirty sky looking for a home that is better than home.

"The judge expressed sorrow at the wasted promise of

a young man's life. A young man who having passively, and by many small steps, found himself in a place where a decision that would cause irreversible harm was almost certain to present itself—this man, the defendant, once that choice was before him, took the course that led to the violent end of another man's life. The judge then sentenced Daniel and I wept as I weep every day. I visit Daniel in prison once every month but before I go I travel south to the cemetery where the guard lies buried. Clive had no family and few friends, and they were just some guys that he drank with from time to time at the corner bar. Clive's sole asset was a policy that paid for a plot, a stone and maintenance, and a Mass that was said at the local church that he had attended irregularly.

"I visit the grave. I don't talk to him. He's dead isn't he? I merely stand and look. I look into the end that I made at one remove, without searching for reasons or consolation. I only want one small thing: to make sure that, while I'm alive, I keep my mind fixed on what happened, on what Daniel did and my part in making it so. That I don't wander away and leave Clive's death smaller, more liminal, more distant than it already is."

Scott shuffled in his seat. Lena gathered her notes together and people all around began putting their books and files away.

"The future doesn't last so long after all," said Sameh.

"Disenchantment is how the game ends. The rules become, not just apparent, but the only visible part of play;

the spirit has departed, the players are brought low and what was spontaneous and jubilant—the broad, chaotic joy—becomes cramped and weakened until the last, fading, playing soul, palms held out, voices the breath of a cry saying 'peace, peace' but meaning 'end me.' The inner light fails. The love of the world that comes through the mouth falls through good to bad, to faint and failing and, finally, to the end of taste and sensation. Oblivion sweeps over obliviousness. The ground beneath our feet has lost its weight, but we are lighter still and the world we made falls silently away fanning the little dust into the tiring sky.

"A woman reaches into a smoking pan and lifts out a buttery baby, the raggy hem of her dress catching fire briefly. She turns and leaves the clearing. The flames die down, the night ends and the baby lies alone in a blanket waiting for the sun to rise and play.

"I have told Daniel that I am no longer going to visit him in prison. I will visit Clive's grave still and wait for my son's release."

The professor stood still looking down at his hands. The slowest of the students finished writing and only then did the bell ring. The door unlocked and the boys and girls ran out into the night calling and laughing and holding hands.

Reading

AT THE RAILWAY STATION an old man approached the bench on which a young man was seated. He stood for an awkward moment crimping his hat in his hands before sitting, bringing close a strong perfume of hay and peppermints. The young man feared that the elder would speak.

He spoke.

"I know something very few people know. There are small occasions of magic still lodged in the world. Books . . . Books are enchanted. Not in the way that people imagine. Not in the sense of wordy transits of delight wrought by restless writers, but something very specific and universal. When you die—when you die—you revive in the world of the last book you were reading before your . . . demise. I can tell that you don't believe me and I don't expect you to, but—because I like you—I wanted to warn you. What are you reading at the moment?"

"*Management Accounting for Non-Financial Specialists* . . . for work."

"That's bad."

"And *Tiresias* by Austin Clarke."

"Ah! That's worse. Poetry is the worst. Never, never, read poetry . . . the torment . . ."

"What are you reading?"

"*Goodnight Moon* and *Three Men in a Boat* . . . but mainly *Goodnight Moon*. Those lovely bunnies. I insist upon an eternity of bliss after what I've been through."

"How did you discover this?"

"I woke up one morning and I knew. Everything I have seen and heard since has confirmed the reality of what I have told you but, of course, on its own none of this proves anything. The original insight is true and gives me peace, although I fear for everyone else in their afterlives."

"But what happens to people who don't read, after they die?"

"Very few people have never read any book or never attempted to read a book. Even the illiterate have sweated uncomprehendingly over the few words of their elementary primers. That will be their book of death. Not such a bad fate."

"But what happens to the 'very few'?"

"They disappear. They die for all time."

"What if they had only read magazines?"

"Magazines, pah!"

"And what happened to the numberless generations born before the book was invented?"

"Well, some of them lived in the time of magic, of which I know nothing, but all the rest are dead for all time."

"That's harsh."

"It's not harsh. It's not anything. It's an opportunity."

"You speak fifteen per cent louder than anyone I know."

"Fifteen per cent? That's not much."

"I suppose so, but it's noticeable. My ears are ringing."

"I'm not sorry."

"You should be."

"Look, I was talking about death and after."

"My mother . . . father always said, 'You're innocent until you die.'"

". . . which is rubbish."

"It might be. If I knew what it meant . . ."

"Well, I can't tell you . . . Anyways. Look. What are you going to read next?"

"*Goodnight Moon?*"

"No! That's my book!"

"What do you mean? You mean that everyone who's reading a particular book when they die ends up in an infinite afterlife together."

"I didn't say it was infinite. I mean, I'm sure it wears out eventually like everything, but I'm supposing that it's a long time."

"According to you."

"Yes."

"So what's the matter with me? What's the matter with spending the afterlife with me? After all you'll have all those leukaemia kids, and toddlers who fell out of windows, and those dads who read the bedtime story, drank the fat end of a bottle of Rioja and crashed into a shop-front on the way to visit their special friends or, on the way back, to buy flowers from the petrol station. To say 'sorry.' All of them."

"Oh! You're right. I never thought of that. How awful! Maybe you could keep me company. You seem all right."

"Thank you. Say: please."

"Please."

"What if you want a slightly more exclusive afterlife? One where you don't have to rub shoulders with Vronsky and a gaggle of lost teenagers."

"You'd have to write your own book . . . and get it published."

"Without anybody reading it? I suppose that must happen already. But I guess the agent and the editors must read it at least. You'd have to spend the afterlife with them."

"You'd have to edit and print it yourself. That's much easier these days."

"What about ebooks?"

"Never heard of them."

The young man could have let the conversation go at this point, it would have been no great loss, but he spoke up instead.

"I've just thought of a foolproof method. Invent your own language, write your ideal post-death scenario in book form, edit, print and there you are."

"You're a clever guy."

"Why, thank you."

"It's a lot of trouble to go to though."

"Yes, well. I'm not saying that I would personally make up a language and et cetera. I've got a better idea."

"Let me hear then."

"Why don't we just act as if there's no path from books into . . . the beyond? We could read anything we want to, even poetry, and never have to worry about it."

"And what if it is true?"

"It might be true but not in the way you think."

"How's that?"

"You might end up in the book and all will be well . . . all the outcomes will be the best possible ones. Raskolnikov doesn't kill his landlady, Werther marries his beloved, settles down and becomes a jolly burgher; Casaubon finishes his book and it's great and everyone loves it, and he lightens up and sees the funny side of things. What does your sense tell you about that?"

"Sounds good . . . might be true."

"Then why don't we act as if it's so and be happy."

"That would be good."

The old man shifted around in his seat.

"Actually, the truth is I don't feel at peace at all. I feel anxious most of the time. I don't sleep well. Great, bloody chunks of doubt float around my mind."

"Doubt?"

"What if none of it is true?"

"Think what you like, something is true and it may as well be an afterlife of happy endings."

"I'd like that," he said weakly.

"It feels like this train will never come," said the young man.

He looked around at the platform, the station. This was the kind of place that usually stinks of urine and bleach, but all he could catch was the faint, soothing smell of lavender.

"This station hasn't been used for ages. There are no trains. I was just looking to have a little rest when I saw you there."

"Would you look at the time?"

The station clock faced them, shattered, handless. "I've got to get to work."

"I wish I'd spent more time in the office. I can't stand my family . . . the ungrateful bastards."

"I'm leaving now."

"Don't leave me," the old man said in a small voice.

The leaving man rushed off the platform and out into the street. A taxi was driving at walking pace down the middle of the road. He flagged, it stopped and he stepped in.

"Where are you going?"

The driver looked familiar. The passenger looked around. Across the street was his workplace.

"It looks like I'm here already."

"That'll be three guineas."

"That's outrageous . . ."

"Three guineas—minimum fare," the cabbie said.

The passenger opened his wallet, took out three notes and climbed out of the cab, leaving the door open. The taxi set off again at a crawl before stopping dead.

The glass double doors of the building were locked and the brass handles secured with a triple loop of chain joined with a brass padlock. He kicked out and hurt his foot and, in a rage, picked up a steel bucket filled with sand, swung it hard and when he let it go the glass shattered. A surge of ecstasy washed through him, stilling any pain or disquiet he might have felt at the blood pouring freely from a cut just below his left eye. The reception was dark and empty, and he walked through over crunchy marble to the atrium where a stand of trees had grown explosively, bursting the canopy, violet and orange blooms singing out of the lush foliage. All the lifts had out-of-order signs, so he took the stairs to the sixth floor where he worked.

All the workstations were closed and tidy except the finance director's whose computer could be seen from across the floor glowing greenly in the gloom. As he approached the desk he smelled bananas. He leaned down to the keyboard and pressed the return key, the screen came back and he had just enough time to read the words "I know something that very few people know" when he heard:

"Kevin . . . Kevin . . . What are you doing here?"

Kevin spun around.

"Hi. Frank."

"You do realise that it's the weekend, don't you?"

"What are you doing here? How did you get in?"

"I have my own key. I mean . . . I've lived here ever since
. . . you know . . ."

"You mean . . . you sleep here?"

"I have a camp bed in the boardroom. The MD has a
shower room that I use. It's all very neat . . . very satisfac-
tory. I miss the kids obviously."

"Naturally."

"I was going to talk to you . . . some Monday."

"About?"

"About what happens when you wake up and you want
to sink to the bottom where the damaged people belong . . .
where you belong."

"Me?"

"No. Me."

"I don't know anything about that and if I did I've
forgotten."

"There it is . . . you remember that there's a forgotten,
you just can't recall what it is. The forgotten is always
waiting for you."

"For me?"

"Yes and for me."

"I don't give it a second thought."

"Yes, but it thinks about you."

"Me?"

"Yes."

"Oh."

"Well, I'm glad we had this talk. I have something to finish. I'll see you on Monday. Bye Kevin."

"Bye Frank."

Kevin walked down the stairs and out into the atrium, the sky had turned dark and the bright blooms had fallen to the ground like rotten stars. Outside a street lamp winked on once, then off, but across the road a warm, welcoming light poured onto the night from a café.

Sitting in a moulded plastic booth smoking a cigarette is the old man from the station.

"Hi Dad," says Kevin.

"I've ordered you a fry, son. It won't be long."

After the Theatre

I HAVE BEEN COUNTING.

There are one hundred and nineteen people out here on the street: not milling, not moving, perhaps happy being still in the warm night air; dressed in gowns and suits, with jewels and bright watches; or in jeans and cotton blouses or checked shirts, acting comfortable. Costumes distinguish others as actors. Musicians hold their instruments, silent.

The theatre is dark and the town lights are down so the sky can be seen. The sea, across the road and over the promenade, rushes similarly towards and away.

My wife speaks:

"I can't remember where I parked the car."

There are no vehicles in the street and I think this beautiful.

She stretches, arms floating upwards, wrists turning above her head, tight fists bursting into fingers, palms facing out white against the blue.

I look at her, as I often do, as if for the first time; and I think how close and unending my wife is, and I think: there is nothing and no one better than she.

She speaks again.

"Did you enjoy the play?"

"It's a beautiful theatre: the red velvet curtains, boxes with golden swags and plaster grapes. When I leaned back to look at the ceiling it was all shadows up there . . . The scenery changed. Twice."

"Each time I really felt as if I had moved."

"People talked."

"The actors. They said their lines. Did you laugh?"

"I'm sure I did."

"Of course, you were beside me . . . I cried as well. At the sad parts."

"Everyone did."

"There was a final act."

"An ending."

Rain falls.

The sea applauds. Everyone is silent.

The marquee of the theatre becomes vastly illuminated. Many crowd forward pushing and pawing at the locked doors.

My wife says, "I don't want to go back in."

The manager speaks up telling everyone it is no use, the show is over, but they keep shoving and shouting, louder, rowdier; a woman cries out, others join her; they stagger back, moaning, making gestures of alarm and confusion. Things are dropped: clutch bags, phones, summer scarves. I leave my wife's side and come closer to the doors to see that another audience has come out into the lobby. There must be an interval.

And there we are, all of us again, in our clothes and faces—well-fed and glossy with life. The smiles are so broad and raw it is as if they were the start of our heads unpeeling. There ought to be worry, a disturbance, but there is only entertainment.

I turn to the street and find that I am alone. The others have gone: out into the darkness.

I forget the show, what I knew of it, and remember the little that makes up who I am. My darling reaches out from the shadows and touches my arm, we pull close, and everything that is left is around me, and we step forward and out to face the sea.

Lights

DOWN HERE, in the lower room, May and I sweat to urge a crate from the ground and out the door. This great, raw wood box could not be heavier if it contained all our worries.

The crate does not contain all our worries.

I am big but I am weak. Long life has taken my strength and left me with joy, and ends, and the knowledge that, wherever I am standing, I am standing slightly to the side of wherever I am standing.

May gives a short eucalyptus cough.

"Michael," she says. "Hunker down."

I get to my knees again and lean my shoulder to the planks, my flesh compresses like soft cheese wrapped in muslin and, as I anticipated, the crate does not move.

May walks to the wall, crouches coiled and tight against the wainscoting and springs forward, her great curly, sunny head preceding her. She hits the crate centrally, with main force. There's a thumping crunch that trembles the world so completely that my teeth fall out. I bend slowly, pick up the gnashers, blow the dust from the gums and plastic enamel and slot them back into my mouth.

"You moved the room but the crate stayed still."

"I can see that you old fool."

"What do we do next?"

May grunts and gestures vaguely to the room, whereupon I lean forward to stirrup her but she leaps over me and lands on the crate. I straighten and look and see her arm extended towards me from above. May tugs hard and I arc through the air and land on my back. The pain is all I could have expected. May kicks me with her soft pink slippers as I roll and scramble about. She stops when I am seated, hugging my knees.

"You can't possibly be hurt." May is right.

I say: "Would you . . . ?"

And I rise and we dance, together not apart, the moves that were old when our parents were young. She is soft and lithe, and her neck and hair smell of cinnamon and honey.

We stop and step back from one another.

May holds me under my arms and swings us into the air. The panels of the crate fall away, raising some little dust, and there is our saggy old sofa, and there are our children as they were in the long ago late evening: immaculate, content, watching cartoons in grey and white, a bowl of popcorn between them.

We are standing in the doorway and I reach for the switch and May puts her hand on mine, gentle, warm, and says:

"It's darker with the lights on."

Golding

EACH TREE HAD A NAME but they did not answer to those
names. In a clearing, in the moonlight, was a cream-
coloured ambulance turned on its side, the doors and
windows open, stretchers scattered all around. Dozens of
men with head injuries wandered about in the lowering
mist. I began to sing and they stopped moving but without looking at me. I was singing like a child. I was singing
like a woman. The words were all one and, as they flowed
out, I struggled for air, but the song would not end and
the melody rose and rose, and I imagined myself pale
blue, growing darker as the clearing grew darker, and I
fell away from the world.

I woke on my feet in the hot white sunlight, still singing.
I stopped. The men moved and they were girls walking
to a hollow where they crouched at a stream and washed
the blood from their foreheads and stood laughing and
set off chasing. Cartwheels were thrown across a carpet
of golden leaves. One did a handstand against a tree;
another scrambled up the girl's ladder body and jumped
from the soles of her feet. She grabbed a high bough and

swung around twice before letting go. In my mind was the twist and snap of an ankle, the crack of a leg, the pop of a knee, but the flying girl landed plumb and straight, gurgling joyously like a much younger child. Others waved their arms and ran across and across each other, fluting and flapping like birds, except they were not birds and could never be birds. And I had been walking all the time since waking and the trees grew closer together, tangled to chest height with spindly bushes that parted as I passed, not scratching but stroking my bare skin softly, and they opened onto the night and a great house in the near distance with yellow light pouring from every window. Breasts swelled under my new blue dress and I felt free as I stepped onto the porch. A man I once knew opened the door as I approached, smiling as he was but unable to talk to me. I looked searchingly at him, trying to find from another time his long black hair and leather jacket, the silver necklace, the charcoal grey T-shirt with the large-winged angel, but he was stooped in a baggy suit and yellow tie, thin hair cropped close to his head, ears fleshier than they were. Shadows had found him and he had fallen in with them.

Piano sounds came down the hall followed by laughter, though the music was sad, very sad. I pushed the door open and the music grew louder. The piano stool was empty. Hundreds of butterflies flew around the electric chandelier, iridescent blue and violet and green, moving near and around but always missing my face. I closed my eyes and the laughter returned and when I opened them the room was full of naked, bloody men lolling on chairs and sofas, smoking cigarettes and drinking brandy. Broken planks warped and cracked in the fire grate. The room was cold. From the flue came the sound of breathing—deep, peaceful respiration. Some men stood and there was dancing.

I walked through a door into a narrow corridor, into a high-ceilinged library. Many of the shelves were empty, ladders reached into the gloom. The books dead birds on the floor. A tree occupied the centre space, rising from the torn carpet. The boughs were fleshy, the twigs, thumbs that twitched, rubbing drily against one another making a hissing sound. I touched my face. The fingers felt too long. They felt a moustache. There was swelling between my legs. The tree stilled. Two thumbs started to snap together brightly. The others joined slowly, at first in unison before shifting apart, clicking across each other contra-rhythmically, louder and louder.

I sat in a chair and listened and questioned whether or not this was music. A coal fire combusted in the fireplace and illuminated the room. Broken toys—tiny cars, a doll's head, a rattle—lay on the slate between grate and fender. I read shapes among the flames and shifting red coals: a wolf's head, a split hand, an odd number of leering eyes; other misshapen anatomies. A woman descended a ladder forwards on her heels, poised by her proper weight.

She held a book open in both hands and wished me a good evening before she sat down near the hearth and read.

There were no dreams. All happened. Senses came from nature but not sense, cause but not action, time but not story. There is, was, only this voice. This, her telling. The beauty of a wet rose. Mine. And a long falling. Mine. A three-fingered stroke across smooth sand or ice or polished oak or dry skin that goes on and on. The new, unowned, perfected impermanence, from home to home, remembering home and home. Blood rains on the glass canopy. The percussion of night. On my hands, ash and newsprint, a heaped fire in the grate, warmth piled on warmth, resinous woodsmoke, warm milk and mace. Soft solitude.

A weary pace.

Days are months is a stalled elevator are years is a frozen pond is a monochrome eye is a nameless, bitter root is a cloud of silica dust is a clutch of cold viscera is a milky glass is an orphaned hand is a spark, infinitely dense and bright, is a shivered dress is an empty chair are first seconds is a milestone, illegible, is wet toffee on the pavement is a filthy ironing board is a calloused foot is a dry seawall is an ember on a rug is a headless statue is a bicycle in a ditch is a small mess of dust picked up by the wind is a shoe mountain is a blank billboard are drums on a bandstand is a teacup trembling as a bus goes by is a radio between stations is the end of a flutter is one corner and another is an unread book, is a read book, is an unread book.

All capacity of knowing, with knowledge itself, runs out and away leaving silence, inside and out.

The flames died down leaving coals glistering momentarily before darkness arrived. I stood up and felt my way through the pitchy air back into the corridor. My leading hand found a handle I had not noticed on my first passage through, which opened a door onto a steep, narrow staircase with a glimmer of light at the top. The stairs narrowed and turned into a half-height ceiling. I crawled into the box-like space and reached a panel at its end that I pounded out with my hand. I rolled into a large day-lit room. A great hairless deer pawed the floorboards, snorting. The deer, not the sun, was the source of the light. The animal's skin, lunar hard and bright, near and distant. My hands itched, my body filled out, my breath heated. I was, I am, I was, essentially, unchanged.

The deer removed its hide and was a man, erect, full-breasted. He dressed, muttering, stood blinking at me, fossicked in a pile of earth in a corner and pulled out a pair of spectacles that he cleaned and polished with a white handkerchief before putting on. Walking across the floor I heard hoof clops. He dipped his head as he exited, I presumed, to prevent his horns from scraping the low lintel. I followed and stepped out onto brown carpet as soft and warm as fresh bread. My limbs loosened and moved more freely. I became aware that I had been suffering from severe pain in my neck, my right shoulder and both my knees; pain which had blissfully departed. He began to run and I took off after him, down the corridor. There was time and more time and salt and ozone and a thick breeze that reached forward and the ceiling shimmered with shifting golden shapes. He dived and hit deep water, shattering into a thousand silver fish that fled apart and gathered into a twisting rope that pulled into the depths.

I hesitated at the water's edge before slipping in backwards. As I swam my clothes melted away, and so too did the hair on my head, my eyelashes and eyebrows, the curls between my legs. The water tasted molasses-sweet, then sour, then sweet again. I drank it up and gagged on a long, scratching object. I rolled onto the carpet at the water's end and spat out a yellowed finger with a bulbous tip. I was cold but ready to begin again.

I moved three strides with each step, the light shifted from orange to green and back again as I opened and closed and opened my eyes. Behind a black leather door was a curtain of chains that rattled as I passed through into a neat red parlour where eight women sat, two to each tiny table, taking tea from willow-pattern china bowls. A naked man with great brick-red limbs and vertical ginger hair came swinging in through a panel door carrying a silver tray from which, with a set of long, rubber tongs, he dispensed biscuits, delicate, lace-like circles, dusted with violet sugar. The butterflies had returned and were circling his head. With a long, sinuous tongue he reached out to their lucent wings but failed to make contact. He laughed, showing an excess of beautiful teeth. The crowd applauded and did not stop, even when he left the room, which made me doubt whether he was the occasion for their approbation. They stopped clapping, hands red and ringing, and their teeth began to chatter. I thought that the women must do everything together always and the ceiling turned black and a glinting grey-blue rain fell in a heavy shower that rattled and skittered off the tables, the walls, the floor—slivers of tempered steel that leapt to my skin and sealed together into a cold casing, that filled my mouth, that cut and choked me. I spat out a little foam of blood and the metal obstacle cleared to let me breathe free. The man ran out, excused himself, and in one generous sweep picked me up in his arms and carried me into the passageway, through a bright kitchen, a storage room, a changing area, a cold room, and into a pan-wash with a double sink and a steamer mounted on stilts that was screwed to the wall. I was dropped with a *clang* and both taps were made to run over my hard body. Some little time passed, the man watching me all the while, and I experienced a pleasant tickling sensation and a gradual softening as I warmed through. I slipped onto the floor and slithered around trying to find my feet. The man departed and returned with a stack of freshly laundered tea towels that he piled on and around me. I stood up and went to shake his hand. He took my hand in his and kissed it forcefully and while he kissed he shrank and he went on shrinking until I lost sight of him and he of himself.

I walked through the kitchen and all the lights were out except those over the hotplates. I narrowly avoided colliding with a bucket and mop and pushed through one set of swing doors and then another, and entered a ballroom. Harsh white light shone from four crystal chandeliers, inverted cones that were clusters of icicle daggers, above their suspending brass ropes and fixtures the ceiling was crazed with cracks, chunks of plaster rose had fallen away. Men and women in fur coats and slippers danced in tight circles, clutching each other hard at the waist, talking in fierce, smiling whispers, their breath visible as fleeting white clouds in the frosty air. On a dais in the corner a woman with short sandy hair stood over two drums, a snare and a tom-tom, with a mallet in one hand and a stick in the other, keeping time without accompaniment. I was invited to take a coat from a rack near the door by a woman in a dirty black tuxedo with a tear at the shoulder. The fur bristled and pulled close around me when I put on the coat. My muscles swelled and tightened and I walked forward with a heavier step into the arms of a woman I knew from when I loved her. We danced and she apologised for being different although she was the same in every important way. Older and fainter of frame but with a vast presence of feeling that was her fragrance.

I apologised for everything and that seemed enough for once.

The drumming stopped, my partner turned on her heels and disappeared into a copse of people who pressed together and bowed their heads. The woman at the door called out that there would be no refreshments on this occasion. Everyone began to leave and I searched for my friend but I could not find her. Soon I was alone and I sat down on the cold, hard floor and cried. When there was nothing left inside I departed, turning into a dark passageway that had a suggestion of light at its farthest end.

I pulled on the handle and the door cracked against its frame. I shoulder-barged the left side. Falling into a large room I saw a blue river rushing from an open sash window across to a fireplace where it hastened into the grate and up the chimney. A person in a white nightgown stood at its bank. She shook her hair and shuddered her breasts, stroked down the wrinkles on the gown's thin material with both hands and dived, roaring bull-like, before hitting the water. I ran over and looked down through the river into the room below. She lay sprawled for a moment before rolling over and jumping to her feet dressed in a three-piece suit, beautifully tailored in brown tweed, with a neat, fat tartan tie. She raised her head to her ceiling, which was my floor, and spoke loudly in my voice but it was indistinct against the water gush and she soon gave up.

The room gave a peristaltic shudder. I ran to the

window and pushed myself into the river against the current. The water threw me back into the room and I landed backwards heavily onto a chair that collapsed in splinters. I rolled on the rug for a moment, unhurt. I stood and returned to the window, narrowed my body and slowly pressed into the warm torrent until it pulled me forward. I fell, turned over and saw the many storeys of the house rise away from me, its pale limestone shone softly, standing as if cut out against the flat bright blue of the sky. I squeezed my eyes closed, saw a dome of stars against a black night, and opened them as I fell into a plantless flower bed. I stood and shook myself dry.

I ran, light-footed on the lawn that boundaried the house and turned into a muddy yard, a quadrangle bounded by derelict stables and a mews. A half circle of lean young dogs watched me, tongues lolling but otherwise motionless. They did not growl as I passed by. I opened, and carefully closed, a wide steel gate, and ran down a narrow, nettle-choked path towards a scrubby paddock where I could see the sky turning orange, and from beyond which came a tidal rushing.

The fields were burning, lit by a too-near sun or a girl with a glass and a star, or a hunter with flint and steel and dry tinder; or none of these things. Yellow, orange, white flames rose and folded and rose again, smoke pillared the way, ash fell in flat flakes that withered and dispersed as they flopped to earth. My mouth filled with bitterness, my eyes stung, pricked and watered but remained clear enough for sight. Birds flew with scorched wings, heading for the lake. Over the fire's mounting roar came the sound of a baby crying, or an otter or a fox or the earth grinding its hard pieces together. My clothes incinerated revealing a cold, wet skin, tarred feathers on my ankles, hard scars ridged and whorled over the rest of my body. The scars and slime saved me. The perishing extended all around as far as the sandstone staircase near the house on one side and the broad water on the other. The burning settled to a loud crackle and I stood in a moment of terminal calm that I felt would have continued indefinitely if I could only have remained motionless. But as I reached the moment of greatest concentration in being still I found that I was walking again, irresistibly moving forward to nowhere in particular.

Ahead was a falling-down shed, around one side of which was a large pen made with long irregular pieces of drift timber. The mud in the pen bubbled and seethed. A woman with waist-long hair turmoiled there, arms and legs thrashing, body twisting, eyes too-wide open, pupils mostly blotting out semi-precious blue. She called out: "I, too, was once a pig." I thought she must be hungry and asked if there was anything I could do for her but she made it clear that she had returned to herself and was content. She stood up, unhooked the gate, walked out into the field and followed the boundary of the deadened fire, the mud on her body baking dry as she went.

Smoke turned and braided in front of me, became a

darker, denser grey, weightier and more present, existent as a rock, just higher and broader than a person. I placed my hand on the cool, gritty surface and felt the regular pounding of a heart. I held it there and focused on re membering what normal might be, for the times when my heart becomes unmoored inside and chooses its own beat, ungoverned by what I need to stay alive.

I looked up and the smoke and dust were clearing, a new sky emerging, cornflower blue mounted with a golden sun. A bridge of white steel arced over the lake, beyond which was a meadow lit with high flames, a pall of black moving towards the distant sea.

There was no longer any green in the world. I stood by the lake hoping for something clean and cool to move through me. The wind shifted the tall reeds, the dry, tangled grass, the beeches and the yews, rustling their few grey leaves, and I swayed lightly rooted as the air pushed and swelled around me. I was a break, an obstacle, though an insignificant one. There was no purpose to me at this time, which was an arrival, a relief and a contentment. There was more here than in other places. The lake and its surroundings felt recalled in that time, now gone, and they persist in my mind and, perhaps, in these few words.

I walked on to a new place. A belly of earth, shoulders of mud, arms broken in pieces and field-flung, with fingers part-buried pointing skyward, treeward, stream-ward, thumbs down. Long hair fussed along a ridge in a breeze, red shoots played around its strands, pools of yellow water reflected the sky. An eye and, elsewhere, another eye, looked up for the gawky crow that would pick and take it on high to see clouds or cliffs or the swinging bough of a blasted tree—the only dead thing around here. A voice had sunk underground to merge with the lightless liquid of the water table but which, following the deluge that ushers in the bright spring, would sound and rise to the surface, frightening all hearing creatures. Stringy organs clung with black, curly hair, hung in the higher reaches of a gorse bush. The ground moved and moved again, the living heart under the pressure of dirt and humus, worms and beetles, threading and weaving roots and sunken water. I thought of what we had done with nature, about the long sequence of reliable, and unreliable, dinners that is history and some of its causes.

I ran seaward. Between two high-banked dunes crowned with sissing marram grass was a depression, a field of stones that receded elliptically away from the highest reaches of the sea: squat blue circles, laid as if by hand, clean and shining on the saltside grading to densely mossed and lichened on the landside. Green: pale and dusty green, black-green, yellow-green, white-green, and yellow, mote-cloud, bright rotten yolk, smear of late summer sun; purple, hovering mauve, bruised heather and night-purple. This space, this lone extent, which could be other places or thoughts or things, was proper as itself. There was no path through. At the margins blew sea violets, fragile and vivid in their personhood. I looked to my own flowering and found nothing but stillness and watchfulness.

I attended to the different sounds around me and found that most of the world's music was percussive, that melody was rare, and consisted of single events or short series, creature-made. The wind partnered with the land, with stream and pool and sea, with the air itself, with vegetation, with the things we made, to make longer, subtler melodies. Trying again to leave off effort made what sounded come together, become music to me, sound happening in time, the notion of it depending on being there. Internal objects and senses changed in response, reached for a harmony that felt like mystery, like harmony.

Thirty-two yellow keys trembled, shook loose from my jaw. I spat them out in triads and a single note and then another note. Gums itched, ragingly so, sharp points tore through the tender pink flesh. Ragged flints, keen-edged, shiny brown and silver grey, filled my mouth. I gasped back blood and stone and bony fragments. I tore at the growths with my hands, slashing palms and fingers. The flint teeth grew long and brittle enough to break off at the root. I cast them into the mud and crouched to wait, watching for growth.

Night fell and was long and wakeful. Hungry birds cried and hunted. Nothing rose. Nothing until a circle of soft domes came pushing up, shining white in the dawn light.

I walked towards the sea, which retreated from me

and as I came on, steadily and then faster, it pulled away, matching and then exceeding my pace. I broke into a chasing run and the waves fled quicker still, roaring out towards the newly risen sun. I laughed and lost my breath, staggered to a halt on the wet sand, grasped my knees and laughed again. The sea had won.

"There has to be a well here," I thought. "There has to be a long fall into water, into darkness. Reaching out at the same distance in any direction, I could touch cold stone walls. Up above would be a crescent of light, next to which would sit a crude wooden lid. Birds would visit the lip but not dare to fly down to where I might be thinking of a well. They would perch nervily, not for my sake but for fear of becoming trapped, flapping and battering against the hard walls that might break their tiny bones. Should birds have such bird-thoughts as these and not other ones. I am the walls, the fall, and the water." And then there was nothing left of my thought of the well except the memory of my face looking down at my face looking up.

I turned back from the coast and walked up the dunes. Through the tall grass of the sandy waste I followed an overgrown path past an abandoned car park and back to the lake.

The lake, broad and black, gently shuddered under a wide breath of air that passed over and over its surface in a wide circular motion. Out of the rushes stepped a woman. The fur on her long coat ran dank water onto her bare feet. In her arms she held a bundle. There was a smell of burnt sugar and soap. The bundle did not move. She placed it on the ground and disrobed, stretched her arms over her head, hands as far apart, fingers as far apart, as they could be. Her skin patched pale silver and green, her body a trunk, diamond-shaped, emerald leaves twisted and shivered out of her branches. A breeze shook her. A boy jumped up from the bundle of rags and ran towards me and kept on running, and I kept on running until I reached the house and opened the door to a kitchen and stopped. A bird sang a two-note song. Once, twice and I stepped inside.

Thoughts were fragrances, felt. Distillate of orange, coffee scent, rose effusions, an insinuating, sewagey gas, the ghost of brackish water, violet smoke, ozone spray, exhalations of sorrow, of joy, pungent confusion. Scents made lights, indirections. All that happened, happens, but matters less and less.

There was deep motion inside the stillness. Tranquillity might have been something in a wider circle outside this, but to move towards it would have been to dispel the present and the possibility of tranquillity and stillness both. The deep motion was change, and many of the possibilities of change, and all that was felt, unaware or just aware of itself, hovering in a place in the body before language. A bird, a small, black, hedge-hopping bird flittered its wings and flew off with the last of my thoughts.

I left for the forest. Lone trees appeared at first. The dry ground cracked underfoot. Green and grey thickened, closer and closer together to make a wood, high above which shivered a canopy that pressed the sun away from itself. I wanted to fall on all fours, to scratch and burrow but lacked the claws and fur. I was a giant, soft white grub. Or that was my mind as I found that, beyond that, I still had arms and legs and the power of forward motion. Men came running through the wood, naked, calling in bird-voices, child-voices, water-voices, tearing at their skin, their hair. Others stood alone talking softly into their hands or playing with their fingers in their palms or their mouths, shining with joy. There was no escaping. No escape for any but me as I could see a break in the trees where a garden grew and a path led out back to the house behind which the sun was setting.

I blinked and stepped and hastened forward beyond the garden, the great steps, the hall, through countless doors and into something like darkness—a long corridor with a mirror at the end. I ran towards myself, standing still in glass: a girl, a dog, a chair, a tired old man who, as I approached, turned back down the reflected corridor a short way and crouched in a darkened doorway. I walked closer and he stood and returned as a woman and we were in our proper positions. I moved and she moved. I was my own stranger.

The room was crowded with furniture, chairs pushed to the wall, not even good for waiting, a fine round wooden table, the dark veneer polished but reflectionless, the scent of beeswax in the air, a cold steel stone, bright in the corner, two doors close to one another. In a long black dress with a black silk waistband, her hair pinned up off her white neck, she stood motionless, looking at her hands or beyond them at some interior object, her back to the soft morning light. Everything was carefully framed for the possession of nothing. There was no voice to call her back. Something passed and there arrived a long extent of something to come: known time, deep time, faint time, felt time. The unheld.

I pulled open a shirt that was around me but I did not recognise and found a body that I did not recognise and watched pathetically the skin's flickering changes from fish white to dull yellow to pavement grey to floating blue-black to sheet white. Blotches appeared, spread, swelled, rashes of full red then tiny white stipples, scatterings of black and yellow and red heads, brown and black moles, nipple-like protrusions along the ribs, a navel pushed out, sucked in—the skin thick and wet and taut, dry and soft and frail. A light shone on the body from an unknown source. A red flower tore out from between two ribs, hot as rage, pushed by a black stem and fell to ground trailing pale, wet roots.

Skin bloated, folded, puckered, sagged. Skin fell away, with the flesh, and the bones appeared, butcherly san-guine at first, quickly white, held up by nothing and finally, falling dust and finally, a vacancy. I closed the shirt that was a plain white dress that fell to just above my knees and I walked to hear the swish. Walked into the dark. Walked, golding.

Cosy

A ROOM, curtains yellow, closed against the gone night and the bright returned sun, walls and ceiling inclined towards one another, corners smoothed, rounded, striped wallpaper, a pattern in soft browns of joined leaves or moths, a black cast-iron fireplace fitted with a gas fire, blond wood set with white heat-resistant teeth, gums and maw painted orange; purple, violet flames murmur steadily throwing out heat, feeding the solid fug. A single bed, a plump, kingsized, cream duvet; a white crocheted cover, loops, knots and knobbles, worn, but cared for. And, in the bed, a man.

George.

George in his own embrace, out of dreams but dreaming, of being exactly where he is: in bed under perfectly weighted covers, out of sight, unneeded, undesirous of movements out or bigger lights or questions that end in ends. Slowly, he cultivates a mild wish to step out into his slippers.

George shifts on his side and pushes against the mattress to raise himself up. He blinks, pushes back his black and silver hair that was slicked and peaked by the motions of the night. He rubs his face: smooth forehead, owlish eyebrows, fleshy nose, large dry lips, salt and pepper chin, jowls and neck. Pinching sleep from his eyes, he presses the bridge of his nose, reaches out to the bedside table and puts on his spectacles. He slides and swings his heavy legs across the sheets and out into the warm, yet cooler, air outside the bed. He lets his feet dangle and inveigle their way, toes twitching, into the tartan slippers waiting on the floor.

George takes an easy pause and stands. There is some stiffness at his ankles that will pass after a number of steps. Fourteen steps. George knows the number. He takes his dressing gown from the chair: black and padded in slanting squares with a red silky interior. Weighty, but comfortably so.

George enters the bathroom and closes the door. He draws back the curtain from the bath, grabs the silver fingers of the tap and twists them almost all the way round. George wets the bristle brush, quickly soaps his face and begins to shave. The mirror ghosts over and he wipes it and shaves under his nose, the mirror hazes and he wipes, and he shaves under his nose. The mirror steams over again. He wipes it and shaves his chin and then his cheeks. He pulls the skin of his neck taut with his thumb on his neck and shaves it in six quick sweeps, his face disappearing in the mirror all the while. He slips the dressing gown onto a hanger and hangs it from the hook behind the door, sloughs off his slippers and arranges himself for a moment beside the tub. George puts both hands on his beige-coloured belly, wobbles it gently and chuckles. He reaches over to the steel bannister for assistance and swings his left leg into the bath, strains up and lifts his right leg and settles slowly, sighing, into and under the water. He spurts and surfaces and swirls off the tap. George reclines, closing his eyes, sighs again, smiles again. If this were all the bliss allowed him that would be all right with George.

His ablutions complete, he pulls the cord, snapping out the light, exits and walks through the bedroom into the hall. A bright, soft, primrose yellow, the light a stamen lives within, the scent faint, clear but discontinuous, of sweet thyme, its dark strands, tiny green leaves, with their variegations of purple, are brought to mind not separately but all at once. He passes picture after picture, each facing its counterpart on the wall opposite, the framing neatly done, the buff paper backing smooth and perfectly sealed. There are no pencilled notes. No studio stickers. No identifying marks of any kind.

The floorboards creak slightly beneath George's feet; the carpet fibres crunch and softly regain their shape as he passes. He descends the stairs and stops at the narrow landing to examine, for the first time that day, his collection of porcelain anchors: buttermilk, cream and whey, the whole dairy spectrum of impure whites, their loops and tines decorated with swirls and stripes of old-wedding-ring gold, new-child's-eye blue.

George moves on from the landing to the last flight. His ring clinks against the bannister curl as he reaches the foot of the stairs. Light passes through crimson glass panels in the front door making the hall rosy. The daily overture ended, slippers shush on the scarlet pile and clack on the tile as he enters the kitchen. The broad, black range still rumbles and purrs from the wood George fed its firebox before retiring to bed. Dense waves of heat enfold him, mildly resinous and amber-heavy.

George takes up the bread knife, the handle warm and worn to silky smoothness, centres the squat white loaf upon its wooden board, settles the blade, blue bright and serrated, on the taut brown crust then moves the knife minutely to the left to arrange a deeper, fatter slice. He saws straight, at first gently, then stronger all the way down to the wood and then again for a second, identical, slice.

George warms the pot and puts freshly cold water on to boil. He places the slices in the toaster, checking the setting before plunging the black lever. He spoons loose tea into the toffee-coloured pot. The water seethes and the kettle rattles, shudders and, finally, clicks, and George submerges the leaves, scalds his cup and, precisely at this moment, the toaster clunks up and he tenderly pinches out the hot slices, placing them onto a warm plate. With a practised hand he smoothes soft butter over each piece, spreading it into every corner, sinking it into the lightly abrasive surface where it glistens lipidly. He dollops marmalade into the centre of the slices and spreads it with the back of the spoon, evenly distributing the orange jelly and heavy-cut pieces of peel. The tray is prepared, with each element—milk jug, teapot, side plate, teacup and saucer, sugar bowl—in its correct quadrant, with a napkin on the side.

George carries the tray through the kitchen to the door of the parlour. He hesitates, feeling his feet settle comfortably, nestle a fraction deeper into his slippers, before he walks into the dunnest, dimmest of his home's rooms. Velvet curtains drape across the window bay in regular purple swags, almost drawn to a close but, at the centre, there is a loose triangle of yellowed lace through which comes an intimation of fierce, naked light.

Above there is a chandelier wrapped in a soft yellow cloth tied to a pendulant hook. On the floor, rug overlaps rug in worn reds, worn blacks and browns, worn greens and flattened patches where the oat-coloured threads show through. A case with a mirrored backing displays the choicest of George's porcelain anchors. Nearby two cases rise from floor to ceiling, filled with books, their spines pushed in to the wall.

The hearth's fire shows only a few patches of orange, but heat pours out of it despite the ash, dark clinker and white slag that have built up around and under the grate, impeding the flow of air. Mrs Noan will arrive tomorrow to clean in her steady, thorough way; no louder than a ticking clock.

In front of the fire is a broad, wing-tipped armchair with three mustard yellow cushions and a tartan blanket in greys and lavender. Flanking the chair on both sides are pedestal tables in walnut, their octagonal edges embellished with golden marquetry. George places the tray on the clear surface of one; a thick leather and brass-bound quarto, its cover studded with precious stones, lies on the other and, next to it, a tiny saucer with a single bead: a forgotten pill.

George grasps the tongs and from the brass bucket builds a coal pyramid, one black slab at a time. Heat rises through the fuel that catches, raising the temperature of the warm air to a swelter.

George crosses the room to an open leather box in a cabinet next to a low table that carries a mid-century gramophone player. He flits with walking fingers through the paper sleeves, selects a record, places it on the spindle and drops the head onto the run-in groove. There is a sizzle and a crack and a softer hiss before piano music begins: a precisely slurred triad and a fainter trailing note, there is a click and the figure repeats and a click and the figure repeats. George smiles and takes his seat.

He pours tea into the cup and begins his breakfast. He finishes his breakfast, wipes his sticky face and fingers, pulls the blanket over his legs and settles. He unsettles and reaches across to the quarto. He lifts its jewelled cover withdraws a pipe, a flopping wallet and a box of matches. He sucks and fills and lights and sucks and sinks back in a cloud of sweet umbrous smoke. The piano plays on.

George smokes for a time. The fire cracks and settles, the air grows still more thick and more torpid. His arm settles onto the armchair's arm; his hands cup the bowl. Gradually, the pipe goes out. The piano plays on.

Legs and arms and torso are first to doze, weighted and weightless, his head next and heaviest, nodding in and out of mind, seeing clouds, inchoate, in and out of sight: blue milk, tobacco haze, a faint, pink demolition shimmer. A gold frame comes into noticing from a near wall, and is gone. His eyes close. His head nods and rolls on his neck. Time goes on in the room without him, with him. There is no difference.

In the dense, soft, wet, flickering place where George is, dreams are happening. His foot twitches. George's painter has slipped its mooring. The skull boat floats away without moving. In his last waking moment there is a part of his mind, perhaps, that is holding on to millions of pages and letting go is what makes him sink or rise into or out to sleep and dreams; dreams sometimes. Dreams that no one knows.

The jaw falls open, the mouth sags, the lower lip rolls down, buttery saliva shining there in its corner. A look of contentment, unknown to itself. A smile with no object. There are liver spots and fine black hairs on the back of his hand—a hand that trembles.

His eyes open.

On the wall is a golden mirror, a painting. A group walk down the canvas on a path of dry, ochre mud, slippers raising dust. The grass, the reeds, the trees around them are sere; all of summer is there always, its radiation caught, held, unmoving. Three girls in white dresses, scarlet traceries embroidered over their breasts, hair braided tightly but coming loose at sly corners; cheeks full and pink in their bronzed faces, the eldest clearly the mother, dipping back into girlhood, grasping a daughter in each arm, laughing, rocking, never to lose them. They might fall, they will not fall; they are swollen with delight, waxing larger in their own gaze. Beyond the wood, the fields, the horizon; a warping line of broken black. George closes his eyes to time.

George rises. He walks until he is standing in front of the back room door. Moisture beads on its green, slick surface. He closes his eyes and leans forward. Heat radiates out onto his face. The bones in his lower back settle and he enjoys an untimed moment of pleasure. George lifts a crabbed hand, a half-fist, and knocks twice. He smiles to himself, pulls down the handle and pushes. Steam gusts and wisps out into the corridor, a loamy scent follows, dense and arboreal. A little grey light seeps into the back room revealing fronds and leaves and little boughs shivering in the formerly dark. There is a chirping, scratching racket, punctuated with monkey cries, unnameable predator growls, high cracks and low rustles. George flicks a switch on the wall and the sound stops, silencing all but the faint hum of the central heating. A moment later and he hears the terse fizz of a humidifier jetting mist into the air. He takes a penlight torch from a hook on the wall, steps into the gloom to examine the plants, and closes the door behind him.

He clicks the torch on, illuminating a large violet-veined, purple bloom with its beam. A sweat of humidity on its satiny skin, it stands out from a dense verdancy, a nesting of fleshy leaves and thin, rigid stalks. George drifts to the scent; a brief electricity dances across his forebrain, accompanied by a relay of light blinking yellow, orange, yellow, and a bitter, grainy taste that fills his mouth. For a moment, some thing or someone is present and unremembered.

George turns to the wall and a white box at head height. He tuts, examining the ridged dial of a timer. He taps the wheel; it clicks and starts to tick. There is a dense *thok* and large lamps thump on overhead, pulsing out a scorching white light. A hiss and the air mists. George hangs the torch on its hook, presses a switch and a shimmering insect chorus begins. He closes the green door.

Peeled and pithed pears, peaches, anise star and cinnamon rod, a little cheap brandy. He sets these to poach in a copper pan on a low heat. George looks through the kitchen window out onto the empty yard: its few square paces of concrete and blackened, red-brick wall. He pulls down a yellow blind at the window. He pulls down a yellow blind at the door. Fruit and spice perfume rise in the air. There is a damp mark on the door blind. As George looks it becomes a something and then almost a word or words, but, just in time, he looks away. He dips and nods over the pan and warms his face, breathing with his eyes closed. There is a moment of inner contraction: everything reducing to an essence that is ripe and soft and sweet, that is full and fragrant and perfectly warmed-through; that is dense and evident and ideal. When the moment expands, disperses, he rises, straightens, the sensation added, to the world George knows.

George leaves the kitchen and walks up the stairs, gasping slightly as he reaches the top, turns into the brown light of the long corridor. The radiators are on full, but the air could be warmer. George thinks of a scarf that he might have worn, and thinks of it again, perhaps in a different colour, and is soon standing in front of a narrow door. He waits. He lifts his hand and lets it hover, thinking about returning it to his cosy pocket, before he grasps the doorknob and twists. Out of the dark comes the scent of burnt dust and lanolin. George reaches inside for a cord near the wall. When he finds it, he pulls, filling the room with red light and harsh heat. The floor and halfway up the walls are plain tiled, there are no carpets or rugs, the window-space is boarded and there is no furniture of any kind. The roof curves and slopes, is covered with row upon row of grille-guarded glowing bars. On the floor in the middle of the room is a typewriter resting on a stack of sheets.

George closes the door, pauses to forget, and begins walking. A few moments later he is seated in his armchair looking, blinking into the fire.

George thinks outside himself for a while. There are evenly spaced rows on either side of a car-choked road. Leafless beeches that shift in place in the chill breeze. Patches that are not signs mark the trunks and boughs in many unnamed greys. A woman's short square heels crack-crack-crack on the pavement. A brown, knee-length, bias-cut coat, green tweed skirt, tan tights, brown oxfords, a deep green paisley headscarf, that might be real silk, tied neatly over her hair and under her chin, its tail taps her between the shoulders with the impact of each step against the street.

She is singing. There is not much to the melody, although it is sweet; the sounds stay mostly in her throat and nose. She takes a large in-breath and starts the song over and now she is smiling, growing larger, maybe denser, firmer, the grey light above and below her becoming whiter. The wind picks up. Leaves and trash circle each other in the gutter, flying out ahead of her, behind her, swirling over the pavement. At the mid-floor of a block of flats across the road, a rag of curtain flaps through an open window. No one is there to close it.

She turns the corner and traverses the narrow, uneven pavement beside a towering box-hedge, its tiny leaves more black than green, its edges harshly trimmed in clean angles. She is walking for a long time and the hedge does not end and then it ends and she turns right into a short cul-de-sac. The houses in the crescent ahead are tall and broad, their pastel, toy-glossy or ice cream colours seem leached out in the winter light. The exception, with its shiny green door and its purple curtains, glowing in the bay windows, would be the kind of place to attract the well-intentioned visitor, even if it were not already where she was set on arriving, on returning to. She walks up the short path and, ignoring a brass bell button, raises her tightly gloved hand and raps the middle of the door.

George returns to himself. The thought and the un-thought expectation of a visitor dissipates in a moment as he realises there really is someone at the door. He laughs and, with a speed that surprises him, rises and strides into the hall. As he passes the convex mirror over the telephone table, George looks and then averts his gaze. He strokes his hair back before turning the deadlock and pulling down the latch. The door opens, the chill air forc-ing its way into the house, and Edith stands there, smile blazing, pulling off her gloves. She leans back, speaking.

"And what are you going to say, George? And what are you going to say?"

She embraces him. They breathe in together and out, and she answers.

"Nothing at all. That's what."

"You must close the door," she said, moving into the open doorway, "all your lovely heat is going. It'll be mak-ing you think, making you want to get on the move. That's where all the trouble starts . . . There's no trouble here."

George steps back and Edith steps in and shuts the door, turns the key in the lock and nibs the latch. Edith removes her coat, shakes off the worst of the damp and hangs it on the one spare hook on the crowded wall-rack. They walk past a cased clock, thin and dark, tickless and tockless.

"You must . . . you must nothing. But maybe you could set that going."

George is looking in her face and starting a slow, sweet smile. "To know the time . . ." she says and George keeps gazing and smiling. She laughs.

"You terrible man, you," and cuffs him gently on the arm, and they go into the front room, Edith first. George has to manoeuvre around her so as not to touch her. He shifts another armchair in front of the fire at a communicative angle to his. The tables have to be moved outwards a little.

Edith remains standing, watching the trouble that George is going to. She walks to the fireplace and turns to the chair, lowers herself slowly, her hands squeaking on the leather arms, her back settling against the seat's back, the cushions exhaling as she does.

"It's a great comfort."

She closes her eyes.

George looks like he might sit down but he stays where he is and waits, hands in pockets.

The fire cracks and shuffles and with her eyes still closed Edith says:

"Tea would be grand, George. And if you've a little something to take the wetness off: a sweet little something . . . I know I shouldn't. We used to say: 'If you don't watch your figure, no one else will.' The girls, that is. We used to say that." George nods and goes into the kitchen, puts the kettle on, fetches two green dishes, places a plain round sponge cake on each, dishes over soft peach and pear and a slop of heat-thickened liquor and, to the side, a large dab of sour cream.

He returns to pour and serve. Edith looks asleep. George adds a half-teaspoon of sugar to her good strong tea and tinks the cup to loose the last drop and she flickers awake, already talking.

"Everything against yourself, it's unequal; you stand out with the simble . . . simple means to hand; smiles, manners, quiet. Or do you? Tea? Lovely. And cake, too. You'd spoil me if I hadn't done the job so well myself."

George snuffles his cake, slurps his tea. Edith takes hers carefully. It takes time; time that neither weighs. There is more tea. Plenty more tea.

Everything is still. Nearly everything is still. The fire repeats itself in cracks and shuffles. Edith has to say:

"Do you remember . . . ? What comes out of the dark when you think of it? It might be something new, that was there at the time, when that time was, but you never noticed it. Was it a detail or something bigger . . . a bigger detail? Or something you made up, whether you knew it or not. Could you put your hand on it? Your fingers through it? I remember those hands, those fingers. The ways you thought about what you needed to do. I take it that you changed their colour and size over the years. That you tore the ways out. Did you? I've kept everything . . . and the discontent."

One hand strokes another in Edith's lap.

"What's perfect is still, isn't it George? That's why I'm such a jitterer, even in my sleep. I've always liked how you don't buzz even when you hover, like most people do—all the calculation still going on, all the striving to matter, to be more than matter. It all tends toward exhaustion in the end. None of us can be protected from wearing out in the end. Even you, George. God, look at you . . ."

She looks into the fire for a moment and then back at George.

"God, love you . . . You never wavered."

George looks into the fire. He laughs into his chest, his face creasing with everything he has known, everything he has done. His lips part. His tongue uncleaves from the roof of his mouth. He speaks.

"I long for the suffering to end."

And laughter streams out into the close air.

DAVID HAYDEN's writing has appeared in *gorse*, *Granta*, *The Moth*, *The Stinging Fly*, *Spolia*, and *The Warwick Review*, and poetry in *PN Review*. He was shortlisted for the 25th RTÉ Francis MacManus Short Story prize. Born in Dublin, he has lived in the US and Australia and is now based in Norwich, UK.

Transit Books is a nonprofit publisher of international and American literature, based in Oakland, California. Founded in 2015, Transit Books is committed to the discovery and promotion of enduring works that carry readers across borders and communities. Visit us online to learn more about our forthcoming titles, events, and opportunities to support our mission.

TRANSITBOOKS.ORG